BLOTTO, TWINKS AND
THE GREAT ROAD RACE

Once again, the plumbing at Tawcester Towers is causing consternation for the Dowager Duchess, so she gives her blessing for Blotto to take part in the Great Road Race in his beloved Lagonda . . . so long as he wins. The first prize of 10,000 pre-War sovereigns will help towards repairing the leaky ancestral home. Blotto elects to take chauffeur Corky Froggett as his spare mechanic, and the team are pitted against Europe's finest in a race that takes them across the Alps to the Colosseum in Rome. Everyone will resort to dastardly deception and fiendish sabotage to ensure Blotto's Lagonda is not the first car over the finishing line. Meanwhile, Twinks is despatched by her mother to the Highlands to paint — and bag herself a wealthy husband, but she's determined not to be left out . . .

BLOTTO, TWINKS
AND THE
GREAT ROAD RACE

SIMON BRETT

LARGE
PRINT

First published in Great Britain 2019
by
Constable
an imprint of Little, Brown Book Group

First Isis Edition
published 2020
by arrangement with
Little, Brown Book Group

A catalogue record for this book is available
from the British Library.

ISBN 978–1–78541–889–1

Published by
Ulverscroft Limited
Anstey, Leicestershire

Set by Words & Graphics Ltd.
Anstey, Leicestershire
Printed and bound in Great Britain by
T. J. International Ltd., Padstow, Cornwall

This book is printed on acid-free paper

To Wilbur,
who writes really good stories,
with love

CHAPTER ONE

Trouble with the Waterworks

"What do you make of this, Blotto me old trouser leg?" asked Twinks.

The real name of the questioner was Honoria Lyminster, daughter of the late Duke of Tawcester and sister of the current one. She stood outside the impressive portico of Tawcester Towers, looking, as was her custom, beautiful. Looking beautiful was effortless for Twinks and, because she never had to think about her beauty, it never seemed important to her. Many amorous swains had praised the perfection of her slender frame, the spun silver of her hair, the delicate contours of her cheekbones and the unfathomable azure of her eyes, but few, when expressing their views, had received a more positive response than a girlish giggle and a cry of "Don't talk such toffee!"

That particular morning, under a sky of cloudless blue, she was dressed in a costume of grey silk whose fringe stopped far enough above the knee to reveal a pleasing amount of white-stockinged leg. The only discordant element in her ensemble was the large black umbrella she held above her immaculate coiffure. Though she stood in the sunlight, its black dome shone with recent waterdrops.

1

"What's tickling your troutlings, Twinks me old carpet-beater?" asked a voice from inside the Tawcester Towers entrance hall.

It belonged to her elder brother, Devereux Lyminster, known by everyone of the appropriate class (and, after all, nobody else mattered) as "Blotto". He was as impossibly handsome as his sister was beautiful. Tall, with the muscular frame of a natural sportsman, this paragon's eyes did not have quite the intense blue of hers, and in him the white blonde of her hair was darkened to a wheaten thatch. That beneath this opulent crop was an almost total vacuum, and that the passage between his two ears was unimpeded by an excess of grey cells, was of no consequence to a member of the British aristocracy. Wherever his brain may have been, Blotto's heart was in the right place, and that was the important thing. When it came to situations where ratiocination was required, he knew he could always rely on the vastly superior intellect of his sister.

"Just pongle out here, Blotters, and you will be lapped around with enlightenment."

As instructed, he pongled out through the massive front doors on to the stone step, where he immediately became aware that he was being deluged by a stream of water. Without moving from the spot, he looked upwards to see the source of this inundation and was rewarded by a cascade into his eyes. He brought his head down again.

"So, what do you make of it, Blotters?" asked Twinks.

"Erm . . . It's raining . . .?" he hazarded, still immobile beneath the shower bath.

"But it's not raining on me," his sister pointed out. "I'm in zing-zing condition out here in the sunshine. So, what do you think's triggered the trickle?"

"Erm . . . A very small cloud . . .?" Blotto hazarded again.

"Not a bad stab for a solution, Blotters. But in it you have ignored one important detail. If you look up . . ." Her brother did so and was rewarded with two more eye-socketsful of water ". . . you will see that the portico has a roof, which no discharge from a cloud could penetrate."

"Tickey-Tockey," said Blotto, again levelling his head, but not stepping away from the waterspout.

"So, do you have another explanation, bro?"

"Erm . . . A very small cloud that has managed to sneak in under the portico roof . . .?" he hazarded. But he didn't sound very optimistic about the validity of the suggestion.

"No. The solution to the conundrum, my old cream sponge, is that the water is not precipitation from the heavens but from a source inside the building."

"Good ticket," murmured Blotto.

"And you know what that means?"

Beneath his continuing deluge, he nodded instinctively. Then he owned up and said, "No."

"It means that there is yet another problem with the Tawcester Towers plumbing."

"Oh, broken biscuits!" And Blotto only said that out loud when things were really serious. Because, short of

3

owning a string of racehorses, there was no more efficient way of pouring away money than trying to keep the Tawcester Towers plumbing in good repair.

"Incidentally, Blotters . . ."

"Yes?"

"You don't have to stand under that waterspout all day."

"Oh, Tickey-Tockey. No, I suppose I don't."

And he moved away from the deluge.

The flow of water in the portico was stemmed by one of the under-footmen, but the repair could by its nature only be temporary. As a famous little Dutch boy found out, there is a finite amount of time that a young man can stop a leak with a part of his body. A more permanent solution would have to be found. A solution that would involve the expenditure of money.

But that was not the immediate concern of Blotto and Twinks. They had plans for the next day.

Blotto wasn't that keen on London. Most of the things that interested him — cricket, hunting and shooting — were available to him on the Tawcester Towers estate, so he was generally happy to give the old Metrop a miss. But he had acceded to his sister's wish — he usually did accede to her wishes — that he should drive her up to Town the following day. Twinks had an appointment with her hair-sculptor, Monsieur Patrice of Mayfair, a man whose handiwork could be absorbed at all events of the London season. Even perfection like that realised in the form of Twinks needed occasional maintenance.

The trip from Tawcestershire and back could be achieved inside the day, so Blotto would not face the unwelcome disruption of sleeping in a bed that was not his own. Also, the journey would give him the opportunity to unleash the full power of his beloved blue Lagonda, frightening peasants off the road all the way up to London and back. So, the journey was not completely without its attractions.

Once arrived at the Metropolis, while in Mayfair Twinks had her locks tweaked, titivated and transfigured by Monsieur Patrice, in St James's her brother could lunch himself indulgently at his club, The Grenadiers, known affectionately to all its members as "The Gren". There he was bound to meet some of his old muffin-toasters from Eton, so the occasion wouldn't be too shabby. Lunch at The Gren always provided some compensation for those more squalid aspects of London — noise, dirt and people.

And, as soon as he arrived in the Marlborough Bar, having dropped off Twinks, his prognostication proved correct. Hardly had he taken the first sip of club claret when he felt a hand smote upon his shoulder and heard a familiar voice saying, "Pippy-pippy, Blotters! How's the old wagon trundling?"

"As right as a trivet's rivet," he replied, turning to see the welcoming face of Trumbo McCorquodash. Though while at Eton the two had shared no match-winning stands on the cricket field, they had shared many midnight feasts. This was a custom which, Trumbo's girth suggested, he had maintained in adult life. His body was so perfectly rotund that his arms, legs and head looked like afterthoughts.

"What can I get you, me old pudding basin?" asked Blotto, turning towards the bar.

"I'm ahead of you," said Trumbo. A podgy hand waved towards a magnum of the club champagne on an adjacent table. "Swill down the red stuff, Blotters, and get stuck into the bubbles!"

Somehow, while they chewed the fat over hilarious scrapes they had shared at Eton, the contents of the bottle seemed magically to disappear. As they moved from club bar to club dining room, Trumbo ordered a second magnum to see them through lunch. "Never drink anything but champagne myself," he confided. "That's how I keep my figure."

There was so obviously no appropriate response to this that Blotto made none. Ordering lunch at The Gren required no great mental effort. Both members knew the menu off by heart, a feat of memory which presented no great difficulty because it offered exactly the kind of food they had eaten all their lives. London's gentlemen's clubs had always provided a great social service in helping their members in that difficult transition from schoolboy to adulthood. This they achieved by offering nursery food, much adolescent sniggering and — most important — no women to alleviate the general level of childishness.

With other of his old muffin-toasters, Blotto's school-day reminiscences would mostly focus on cricket or hunting. But since Trumbo McCorquodash's only possible role in the game had been usurped by the ball, and his tendency to roll off horses disqualified him from the pursuit of the fox, their conversation homed in on other topics. One unfailing source of mutual interest was the internal combustion engine. Along with his trusty cricket bat and his hunter Mephistopheles, the final part of Blotto's triptych of adoration was his Lagonda. And Trumbo McCorquodash prided himself on a whole fleet of powerful cars, all of them boasting customised seats to accommodate his considerable bulk. So, their journey through pea soup, shepherd's pie with three veg and rice pudding was enlivened by discussion of carburettors, differentials and gear ratios. There was much talk of torque. And, before long, Trumbo got on to the subject of his latest acquisition.

"Lovely Bentley six-and-a-half-litre. Overhead camshaft, four valves per cylinder — and the single-piece engine block and cylinder head is cast in iron, which of course means . . .?"

"You don't need a spoffing head gasket!"

"You're bong on the nose there, Blotters! You still motor-munching with the Lagonda?"

"Yes, by Wilberforce! Old girl remains as jammy as a cream tea."

"She'd never thrash the Bentley on a straight run, though."

"Oh, come on, Trumbo, you're jiggling my kneecap. A Bentley may have a bit of oomph, but it's as heavy as a Mark IV tank. Drives rather like one, too, I've heard along the birdwire."

"You're pulling my pyjama cord, Blotters! The Bentley'd scrunch the Lag into a used cigarette paper any day."

"Trumbo, you're talking absolute globbins! Two minutes from a standing start, the Lag'd leave the Ben just a dot on the horizon."

"A dot on the horizon in front, not behind."

"You're talking through your elbow patch, you old trout-tickler!"

"Well, come on, Blotters, let's put it to the bench. Side by side, level start, Lag and Ben, one mile flat. Are you up for the tiddle?"

"Am I up for the tiddle? Toad-in-the-hole, you've got a taker, Trumbo!"

"Well, I'm gathering up your gauntlet. Name your terms. Where and when?"

"No point in shuffling round the shrubbery. What's wrong with now? That magnum of the bubbly stuff has really set me up for a bit of driving. And what say we do the race down Pall Mall?" Blotto's rather limited imagination could not envisage a more attractive way of passing an afternoon in London.

"Ah." A shadow crept across Trumbo McCorquodash's moon face. "Bit of a stye in the eye there, I'm afraid."

"Oh?"

"Haven't got the Ben with me. Came up to the Metrop on the choo-choo."

"That's a bit of a candle-snuffer. Still, no use crying over slopped champers. Have to rebook the fixture. There's a nice bit of open road on the way back to Tawcester Towers. We could set the stumps up there."

"Good ticket. Is it an open stretch?"

"You bet your knee-hairs it is. We could use both carriageways. Might be a bit of traffic going the other way, but only boddoes like farmers and commercial travellers, so they'll get out of the way if they know what's good for them. And if they don't . . . well, no skin off our bones."

"Sounds a real buzzbanger of an idea, Blotters . . ." Excitement spread across Trumbo's round face as a new thought came to him. "Unless of course you fancy putting the motors to the test over a rather longer course . . ."

Blotto's fine brow furrowed, as if in thought. "Sorry, not on the same page?"

"I heard recently, from a bunch of ne'er-do-wells I mix with over the nags, about a Great Road Race."

"Toad-in-the-hole! What's that when it's got its spats on?"

"Some merry thimble's setting up a Great Road Race across Europe. Bullies off in Trafalgar Square, then the motors zap down to the South Coast, ferry to France, and from there I gather it's non-stop through Europe till the chequered flag in Rome!"

"Sounds a beezer wheeze, Trumbers."

"Going to be an international line-up of steering-wheelers. Boddoes from all over the world trying to prove their speedsters are better than ours."

"No chance! Not one of those garlic-guzzlers could beat the Lag — or even the Ben, come to that."

"If we both do it, Blotters, we can have a private side bet on which one of us finishes first."

"Well, we could," Blotto conceded, "but I'd feel bad about making off with your jingle-jangle."

"Huh. I'll take yours without quibble or qualm. In fact, might be simpler if you write me a cheque right now, because I know it'll be the Ben that biffs it."

"Puddledash! The Lag could coast it with one wheel tied behind its back."

"Anyway, whoever does cross the finishing line first won't be hard up for the odd spondulicks."

"Oh?"

"There's a lot of golden gravy at stake. In fact, the prize for the winner is ten thousand of the King's best smackers, to be presented in the form of pre-War sovereigns."

"Toad-in-the-hole!" said Blotto. "Where does a boddo sign up?"

CHAPTER
TWO

The Dowager Duchess Gives
Her Orders

There were cliffs and bluffs all over the world which had proved intractable challenges to international rock-climbers, but none was craggier than the features of the Dowager Duchess of Tawcester. When she was in a bad mood, they would have frightened off even the most tenacious of mountain goats.

And she was in a bad mood the following morning in the Blue Morning Room. Its cause was yet again the Tawcester Towers plumbing. Though a rota of under-footmen had been established to stem the flow in the portico with their bodies, she knew that could only be a temporary repair. Since the demise of the feudal system — a development which the Dowager Duchess regarded as an unmitigated disaster — there was a limit to what could be demanded of the servant class. As the poison of Socialism spread, some of them even reckoned that they had rights of their own. All of which meant that money would be needed to provide a more permanent solution to the plumbing problem.

So that morning was not an auspicious time for Blotto to propose an enterprise which would put a further drain on the estate coffers. He was glad Twinks was present to give him moral support. He had summoned his sister from her boudoir, where she had been working on her latest intellectual project, a study of aviation. She was particularly interested in the virtual lift-off machines being developed under the name of "helicopters", and the (literally) ground-breaking work in that field by Jacques and Louis Bréguet, Paul Cornu and Jacob Ellehammer. But, when her brother needed her, Twinks had happily put her research to one side and set off with him towards the Blue Morning Room.

"A Great Road Race?" the Dowager Duchess echoed, adding a lavish layer of contempt to his words.

"Yes, Mater. I heard about it from Trumbo McCorquodash. You remember Trumbo?"

"Second son of the Earl of Godalming?"

"You're bong on the nose there."

"Bearing more than a passing resemblance to a barrage balloon?"

"That's the Johnny."

"If he's anything like his father, he's a terrible spendthrift. There wasn't a tradesman in London he didn't owe money to. Is the son the same?"

"Yes, I'm afraid Trumbo can be a little splash-happy with the old jingle-jangle."

"Don't apologise, Blotto," his mother boomed. "As you should know, debt is the mark of gentleman."

"Couldn't agree more, Mater." He smiled, encouraged. "So, if you don't mind me building up a bit of debt, I'm sure my entry into the Great Road Race will be —"

12

"I didn't say that, Blotto. In this household, there will be no excess spending until the plumbing's fixed!"

"Oh, but, Mater . . ." Many supplicants in such a situation might have completed the sentence: "have a heart." But, since Blotto knew his mother hadn't got one, he didn't bother.

"Tell the Mater more about the set-up of the race," suggested Twinks.

"Yes, do," said their mother. "Is it being arranged by a respectable person?"

Blotto had got more information on the subject from Trumbo McCorquodash and other Old Etonian friends, so he was able to reply, "The brainbox behind it is an automobile manufacturer."

"Not a respectable person then," the Dowager Duchess observed.

"Very successful automobile manufacturer," Blotto countered. "Very reputable."

"Blotto, was all that money lavished on your education wasted? Surely you know that a motor manufacturer can never be 'reputable'. A motor manufacturer is, by definition, in trade."

"But this company's quite famous. Called Carré-Dagneau."

" 'Carré-Dagneau'?"

"French."

The shudder which ran through the Dowager Duchess's massive frame was more articulate than any words could have been.

"Yes, Mater, but that's just the organising oiks for this Great Road Race. For the driving wallahs, Trumbo's enlisted quite a line-up of our old muffin-toasters from Eton. British too. Not a garlic-cruncher amongst them, the ones he's dragooned in." Blotto didn't feel it was the moment to mention that a good few of the other competitors were foreign. "Most of the boddoes who're entering have pages and pages devoted to them in *Burke's Peerage*," he pleaded.

His mother produced a "Hmm" sound, which was as near as she ever got to conciliatory.

Blotto pressed home his advantage. "Besides, it's a point of honour . . ."

'Point of honour'? his mother echoed. She was always interested when situations involved honour. "A point of honour for you, Blotto?"

"I was thinking more of a point of honour for the Lag."

"Oh?"

"Well, look, the reason the Carré-Dagneaux are putting their beef into the pot on this one is that they're launching a new model. Seven-litre roadster called the 'Florian'. They reckon if their little judderer wins the Great Road Race, customers'll be all over their showrooms like the measles."

"Blotto," the Dowager Duchess pronounced, "I do not have the smallest inkling of what you are talking about."

"The Carré-Dagneaux think they're going to win the race, which will not only be good for their trade . . ." His mother winced at the word ". . . but will also mean the prize money goes back to them. Which is why it'll be a point of honour for me to prove the Lag is a better motor than the Florian — or indeed any other petrol-pumper. And I know the Lag's way beyond the —"

"Cease to speak, Blotto!" He did as instructed, having known from the cradle onwards that, in any dealings with his mother, instant obedience was invariably the best course. "Did I hear you use the words 'prize money'?"

"You're on the right side of right, Mater. That's exactly what I said."

"And how much is this prize money?"

"Oh, can't put a finger on the figure," said Blotto, to whom such details were unimportant. "Ten thou I think it was."

"Ten thousand pounds?"

"Tickey-Tockey. Ten thousand portraits of His Maj on pre-War sovereigns." He stopped for a moment as a new thought came to him. "Of course, it'd only be ten thousand actual coins if they did it in oncers. If it was fivers or termers, then it'd be —"

"Silence, Blotto! Are you saying that, if you, in your Lagonda, were to win this Great Road Race, you would be in receipt of a ten-thousand-pound prize?"

"You're snuffling towards the right truffle there, Mater. That's exactly what I'm saying."

"And you say the Lagonda can't lose?"

"Hasn't been a bigger cert for the bookies since they closed the book on the name of the next King."

"Hm." The Dowager Duchess looked thoughtful. "So, Blotto, were I to agree to your participating in this Great Road Race . . ."

15

"Yes, Mater?"

"You would be guaranteed to return here to Tawcester Towers with ten thousand pounds."

"Well, I suppose I could do."

"What do you mean?"

"I will win the race — no wobbles about that — but of course I won't come back with the money."

"Why not?"

"Well, come on, Mater. Gentlemen and Players and all that. Someone of my breeding can't accept money for playing sport."

"Blotto," said the Dowager Duchess in the kind of voice Moses used when he raised his staff to frighten off the waters of the Red Sea, "if you are expecting the Tawcester Towers estate to fund this expedition for you, you will not only win the race, you will also bring the prize money back here!"

"Tickey-Tockey, Mater," he replied, though it went against his instincts as a sportsman and a gentleman.

"You will bring the money back here, and it will be used to sort out the plumbing."

"Tickey-Tockey, Mater." Blotto was subdued, then slowly he realised that his mother had actually given him permission to take part in the Great Road Race. Like sunlight creeping across a cornfield, a beam illuminated his impossibly handsome features. "Toad-in-the-hole!" he said.

"Practical matters . . ." the Dowager Duchess boomed. "When will you leave? Will you be on your own?"

16

"Haven't got the full SP from Trumbo yet, but I know the bully-off in Trafalgar Square is in a fortnight's time. And I imagine the whole clangdumble would take about a week. End of March. Which is a bit of a candle-snuffer, because it means I'll miss the opening of the cricket season."

"And would you be doing the drive on your own?" asked his mother.

"Have to check the rules and regs on that. But I'm sure you'll be allowed a mechanic. As to who it is who pongles along with me . . ." He was unaware of the frantic eye-signals his sister was flashing at him. "Well, I'm going to need someone who knows the Lag inside out, so I'll take Corky Froggett."

"Corky Froggett?"

"One of the chauffeurs, Mater."

"Oh yes," she said dismissively. The Dowager Duchess could not be expected to know the names of all the staff on the Tawcester Towers estate. Or any of them, come to that. For her they were just interchangeable peasants. "That would be acceptable."

During the last exchange, the semaphore from Twinks's azure eyes having had no effect, she cut directly to the chase. "Mater," she said boldly, "I think I should go with Blotto."

The Dowager Duchess faced her down with a look that would have melted tungsten. "And what possible reason could there be for you to accompany him, Honoria?" The use of her daughter's full name was a measure of her disapprobation.

"Well, Mater, on an expedition of that sort, Blotto's bound to get into some pretty gummy scrapes." Her brother nodded. How well she knew him. "And from the nursery onward, I've always been a whale on getting the Bro out of gummy scrapes, haven't I?"

Another nod from Blotto. He hadn't needed much convincing, anyway.

It was perhaps unsurprising that their mother saw things differently. "Blotto will have with him this chauffeur, Froggy Corkett." Neither of them had the temerity to correct her. "That should provide sufficient protection from his worst idiocies."

"Mater, I'm sure I could help with —"

"Silence, Honoria! The subject is closed."

"But, Mater, I do need a bit of time away from Tawcester Towers, just to —"

"Do not argue! The only possible reason why you should leave Tawcester Towers is to speed up your chances of finding a suitable husband. And what kind of husband material is likely to be found among the contestants in a Great Road Race?"

"Well, it's possible that —"

"Honoria! My question was rhetorical. I refuse to allow you to accompany your brother on this expedition!"

Twinks looked subdued, without being surprised. Her mother's proscription was an eventuality for which she had prepared. "I wonder then, Mater, if I could go away somewhere else during the week that Blotto is participating in the Great Road Race . . .?"

"Somewhere else? Where else?"

"I have read of educational courses for young ladies . . ."

"'Educational courses'? Honoria, you have been perfectly adequately educated — for a girl. You know how to dance, ride a horse, simper and dress yourself — with the help of a maid, obviously. What other possible educational needs do you have? Never forget, girl, that education in a woman *puts men off!*"

"I am aware of that, Mater." The Dowager Duchess knew nothing of her daughter's exceptional intellectual powers and achievements. Twinks was very happy that things should stay that way. She moved forward with her prepared plan. "I would wish you to know, though, that some of these 'educational courses' have proved fertile ground for the development of attachments which resulted in matrimony."

"Oh?" Twinks had the Dowager Duchess's full attention now.

"Lalage, daughter of the Earl of Chippenham, met her future husband, son and heir to the Duke of Wrexham, during an educational course on the tying of salmon flies."

"Did she, by Wilberforce?"

"While Laetitia, second daughter of the Marquis of Hartlepool, recently married the Earl of Lytham St Annes after meeting him on a course where they were learning to mix cocktails."

"This sounds extremely promising. And where do these 'educational courses' take place?"

"That's what's so creamy éclair about the whole clang-dumble, Mater. They take place in the houses of the aristocracy."

"Oh?"

"Yes, some of the other denizens of Debrett's, finding themselves a little short on the old jingle-jangle front, have taken to renting out their premises for capers of this kind."

"Renting out their homes? For money?" asked the Dowager Duchess, appalled.

"Yes, Mater."

A shudder to rival the eruption of Krakatoa ran through the Dowager Duchess's body.

Blotto, still not quite able to square his mind to the idea of taking the Great Road Race prize money, saw an alternative solution. "Maybe, Mater, we could do that? Get the spondulicks to sort out the Tawcester Towers plumbing by renting out bits of the old hovel?"

The look his mother turned on him would have deforested Brazil. "Blotto," she fulminated, "don't be so inexpressibly vulgar." She turned her steely gaze on her daughter. "And in the home of which *déclassé* aristocrat does your proposed 'educational course' take place?"

"Craigmullen."

"I am not familiar with the name."

"In the Highlands. Not far from Inverness."

"Oh," said the Dowager Duchess, with considerable relief. "We are speaking of *Scottish* aristocracy. Well, of course, one does not have such social expectations from people of that kind."

"What's more . . ." Twinks hastened in to widen the chink she had observed in her mother's wall of opprobrium. "It's the ancestral home of the Dukes of

20

Glencoe, who own all the bits of Belgravia which don't belong to the Duke of Westminster."

"Really?" said the Dowager Duchess, her interest now seriously kindled.

"And I happen to have heard, from a bijou birdette of my acquaintance, that the Duke of Glencoe's son and heir will be present at Craigmullen at the time of the educational course which I am proposing to attend. And also, to put the cream on the crumpet, he is unmarried."

Another seismic contortion of her face demonstrated the Dowager Duchess's best attempt at a benign smile.

"Then, of course, Twinks . . ." The use of the less formal name might suggest some thawing in the permafrost of the Dowager Duchess's demeanour, ". . . you absolutely *must* go to Craigmullen. I should remind you, however, that people in our position should be very careful how far we go down the 'educational' route. Tying salmon flies and mixing cocktails are all very well, but it doesn't do for people like us to be seen to be learning anything that might be *useful*. What kind of educational course were you planning to enrol in, my girl?"

"Water colours, Mater."

" 'Water colours'? What, you mean . . . *Art*?"

"You're bong on the nose there, Mater."

An unwonted subterranean movement shuddered through the tectonic plates of the Dowager Duchess's expression. This was yet another attempt at producing a smile. "That is excellent news, Twinks. You may go husband-searching on such an educational course with my blessing. It is well known among people of breeding that Art has never proved even mildly *useful*."

CHAPTER
THREE

Consultation with Corky

"France, eh, milord?" Corky Froggett's moustache twitched like the nostril of a hound that's just caught a distant whiff of fox. Though devoted to the Young Master and to his duties at Tawcester Towers, the best time of the chauffeur's life had undoubtedly been in the trenches during what he referred to as "the recent little dust-up with the Hun". War could have been designed for someone like Corky. He was a highly efficient killing machine, who resented that his skills were not only unwanted, but also illegal, in peacetime. How he missed having a licence to shoot Germans — and the occasional Frenchman who got in the way (he wasn't fussy).

"Yes," Blotto confirmed. "Through France and down into Italy. The whole clangdumble finishes in Rome. And of course, the Lag's going to win."

"Of course, milord." Corky would never have considered any other outcome.

"The other entrants have about as much chance as a tutti-frutti in a furnace."

"Rather less than that, I'd say, milord."

The two men chuckled. When it came to talking about cars, there was no master and servant; they were just a pair of enthusiasts, heady on the fumes of petrol. They stood in one of the Tawcester Towers garages, one each side of the Lagonda's long blue bonnet, both looking down as if at the contents of a manger in Bethlehem.

"So, anyway, Corky, what this means is that I need this baby tuned up as tight as a fiddler's bowstring — or do I mean an archer's G-string?"

Corky looked affronted. "I wouldn't know, milord. But I would like to point out that I see to it that the Lag is always tuned up as tight as a tailor's tick."

"Oh, Tickey-Tockey, Corky. I know you do. I just meant this time we're going to have to pull out all the crank-rods. We can't let ourselves be beaten by any of those foreign boddoes."

"I'm sorry, milord. I was not aware that persons of a foreign nature would be competing in the race." Corky's moustache twitched again at the thought of conflict.

"Oh yes, quite a few, I think. Twinks is doing a bit of research on them, getting the SP, as it were. She says there'll be a whole roll-call of garlic-guzzlers, sausage-stuffers and pasta-poppers on the starting grid."

"In that case, milord," Corky Froggett assured him, "if there are foreigners involved, I will see to it that the Lag is tuned to a level of perfection hitherto unseen in the annals of motoring history."

"Good ticket, Corky! That's the Johnny!"

"There is one thing, though, milord, which I would wish to draw to your attention . . ."

"Well, come on then, uncage the ferrets."

"It is a matter we have discussed on previous occasions, milord. The compartment which was attached to the vehicle's chassis while we were on the wrong side of the Atlantic."

"Ah, good biff from the brainbox, Corky. I'd forgotten about that." During a sojourn in the States, attempting to put into practice the Dowager Duchess's idea of marrying Blotto off to an American heiress, the Lagonda had suffered the indignity of being captured by the Mafia. They had had the temerity to add to the vehicle an under-body storage space, suitable for the secret transportation of two men or two corpses, as the need arose. On previous occasions, the removal of this ingenious facility had been discussed between master and chauffeur, but each time the decision had been made to leave it in place. And the compartment had proved its utility on more than one occasion for the transportation of such commodities as gold bullion.

Blotto went on, "I must lace up my thinking boots on this one. By how many of the old m.p.h. do you reckon the compartment slows the Lag down?"

Corky Froggett's brow wrinkled. "Depends on whether it's full or not. When it's empty, doesn't make too much difference, not a lot of drag from the wind. The Mafia," he conceded grudgingly, "did a good job on that. You planning to put anything in the compartment, milord?" Blotto shook his head. "Then you should be all tickety-boo ... We keep the compartment in place and still leave the also-rans gasping . . . depending, of course, on the opposition we're up against."

"Well, I've said some of the boddoes will be foreigners."

"No worries about them, milord. British engineering is the best in the world. I was more worried about the home competition."

"One of the entrants is an old muffin-toaster of mine from Eton. Trumbo McCorquodash."

"And what'll he be driving?"

"A Bentley."

"A Bentley?" Corky Froggett almost doubled up with laughter. "We've got no worries there, have we? A Lag that's got a wheel missing'll beat a Bentley any day of the week."

Blotto stroked the car's bonnet as gently as a mother might her firstborn after it'd been saved from drowning. "Anyway, Corky, I'll trust you to get this breathsapper into zing-zing condition by Sunday week. That's when the starting pistol will be fired in Trafalgar Square. You'll have it up for that?"

"I'll have her tuned like a Stradivarius," the chauffeur replied. He didn't know what a Stradivarius was, he'd just heard the expression used. From the name, though, he reckoned it must be a foreign make of car.

Blotto made no comment. He didn't know what a Stradivarius was either.

"Get this down you, Blotto me old bottle-brush." Twinks handed him a cup of cocoa, took a sip from her own and draped herself elegantly over a *chaise longue*. They were in her boudoir, where they frequently indulged in evening cocoa.

The boudoir was Twinks's private domain, where she performed, sometimes with the help of her maid, those secret feminine rituals which made her look breathtakingly beautiful every time she left the room. It was also her library and study, where she worked her latest intellectual challenge. It was there that she had completed her translation of Dostoyevsky's *The Idiot* into Sanskrit. And written her definitive paper on the use of hydroelectric power in slum clearance. It was also in her boudoir that she had worked out the first successful proof of Fermat's Last Theorem (though she had not told anyone about her solution, because she thought it was too obvious to be worthy of interest).

Because of her researches, the elegant room was always full of books, of which Blotto, as he did with all books, took no notice. Had he looked at the ones spread over her dressing table that evening, he would have discovered that his sister's latest obsession was with aviation, and particularly with the development of vertical lift-off aeroplanes. Had he explored further, he might have found the empty stable on the Tawcester Towers estate where Twinks was conducting practical experiments with her aeronautical inventions.

But, recognising the inferiority of his own, Blotto never bothered himself too much with what went on inside his sister's brain.

He watched as she reached into her sequinned reticule and produced a small, silver-backed notebook.

She extracted the silver propelling pencil from the slot on its spine and smiled across at her brother. "Well, I've been doing my research, and you've got a proper League of Nations lining up for next week's Great Road Race frolic."

Blotto didn't say anything, just waited for the ferrets to be uncaged. When Twinks did her research, she really did her research.

"Right, tune up the brainbox, Blotters. Be useful if you remember all this guff. And I'll start with the French, since they're stumping up the mazuma for the whole hockey match. The Carré-Dagneaux are running the show."

"I did actually tell you that, Twinks," Blotto pointed out.

"I know you did, but I've found out more about the setup. The firm's been on the ledgers for quite a while. Started by the Pater of the current proprietor, who milked the market for the bicycle trade. Made a mint, which he then invested in the internal combustion engine. When he tumbled off the trailer, he left a thriving money-mill to his son, Monsieur Jean-Marie Carré-Dagneau."

" 'Jean-Marie'?"

"Yes."

"But 'Marie''s a girl's name."

"But in France they quite often —"

"Toad-in-the-hole!" said Blotto. "If I ever met a boddo with a girl's name, I'd definitely get the feeling the Stilton was a bit iffy."

"As I say, it's quite common in —"

"I certainly wouldn't want to go through life called Devereux-Dorothy or something like that."

"Blotto, there's no danger . . ." Twinks gave up. Some of her brother's trains of thought were just not worth catching. Let them find the sidings on their own. "Anyway, Jean-Marie Carré-Dagneau's wife is called Adélaïde."

"What in the name of strawberries has his wife got to do with anything?"

"She has quite a lot to do with everything, as it turns out. Though it's Jean-Marie Carré-Dagneau's name printed at the head of the paper, Adélaïde's the one who decides the content of the letters."

"Tough old rusk, is she?"

"Tough as a gamekeeper's britches."

"Tickey-Tockey."

"And she's the one who wears the britches too. Jean-Marie stands up to her like a hankie in a hurricane. He gives her whatever she asks for. And a lot of what she asks for benefits their son Florian. The boy is more than the apple of her eye, he's the whole spoffing orchard of her eye."

"Oh. Florian? Same name as their latest car. Coincidence, what?"

"No coincidence, Blotters. Adélaïde demanded that the car be named after the boy and, as ever, her husband agreed. What's more, she's insisted that the little spongeworm should drive the thing in the Great Road Race."

"Toad-in-the-hole! And does this Florian have much experience in the old road-racing game?"

"For the last year, the young man has been having lessons."

"Lessons?" echoed a shocked Blotto.

"Yes. From one of France's most experienced racing drivers."

"Oh?" Blotto was even more shocked. "Well, that's way outside the rule book, isn't it?"

He didn't need to explain more. Twinks fully understood. British sportsmen were sportsmen by instinct and divine generosity. Practising for any kind of sport . . . or, even worse, training . . . were the marks of the foreigner and the cad.

"So," he went on, "it looks like the filchers are investing a fair wallop into the whole shooting match."

"You've potted the black there, Blotters. They've got big bets on the back of this one. They're determined to win, not only to ginger up the sales of their new motor, but also because Adélaïde always wants her precious little goo-goo to win everything. So be on your guard, they'll be up for any backdoor-sidling."

"You're slapping it on with too thick a brush there, Twinks. We're talking about road-racers here. Drivers are honourable boddoes, always on the right side of right."

"Even when there's ten thou in gold sovs up for the grab?"

"Even then."

"Blotto," Twinks reminded him gently, "the people under discussion are French."

"Ah yes. I read your semaphore. The stenchers have never forgiven us for Agincourt, have they?" He referred to a battle at which the Lyminster family had been well represented. "Good ticket, Twinks. I'll keep the peepers peeled for any shifty shuffling from the Carré-Dagneau family. But there's no one else I have to don my worry-boots about, is there? Most of the also-rans are my old Eton muffin-toasters."

"There are still a few other rats in the larder, Blotto."

"Oh."

"One of the entrants is German."

"A sausage-stuffer, by Denzil!"

"Give that pony a rosette! Yes, his name's Count Daspoontz. He was an air ace during that last little dust-up between our two countries, brought down some fifty British wing-warriors."

"Can't hold that against a boddo. War's just a game, like any other, and so long as he played by the rules . . . well, fair biddles to him."

"According to my research, you still shouldn't trust this particular filcher further than a thuggee's thumb."

"Tickey-Tockey, Twinks. What's he driving?"

"The new eight-litre Krumpfenbach."

Blotto let out a low whistle. "That's some bit of ironwork."

"Trouble the Lag?"

Blotto beamed. "Nothing troubles the Lag, Twinks me old porridge-scraper. Any other migrants from foreign climes in the line-up?"

"Apparently, there's an Italian combo."

"Driving what?"

"A Fettuccine roadster."

"Nippy little kettle, I've heard."

"Challenge for the Lag?"

"Oh, come off it, Twinks. You're jiggling my kneecap. Nothing's a challenge for the Lag."

"Well, I'm sure you and the Lag will soon be lighting the fireworks of fun in Rome."

"Tickey-Tockey, Twinks me old saucepan lid." Then, thinking he might have detected a hint of wistfulness in her previous sentence, he said, "Wish you were coming with me . . .?"

A toss of her head shook away introspection. "Oh, don't don your worry-boots about me, Blotto me old collar-starcher. I'll be lighting my own fireworks of fun at Craigmullen."

"Good ticket. Yes, doing your course in . . . erm . . . Could you give the old memory a jiggle?"

"Water colours."

"Righty-ho." There was a silence, then Blotto said, "Always wanted to ask this, Twinks me old banana-straightener . . . How do you colour water?"

CHAPTER
FOUR

Under Starter's Orders

"I received a telephonic communication this morning, milord," said Corky Froggett, as he navigated the Lagonda through the encroaching suburbs of London. Initially reluctant to hand over the steering wheel, Blotto had been persuaded it would make sense to conserve his energies for the road-racing challenge of the days ahead. Rather than sitting in the back, as his rank might have required, he was in the front passenger seat.

"Did you, by Denzil?" he responded with some surprise. The telephone in the draughty hall of Tawcester Towers was used chiefly by the Dowager Duchess as a means of bullying junior aristocratic acquaintances. It was rarely that a call came for anyone below stairs.

"Yes, milord. It came from a functionary of the Carré-Dagneau company."

"Oh? No kinks in the fly line over our entry for the race, I hope?"

"No, milord. They did, however, point out that we were not taking advantage of all of the facilities which the rules of the Great Road Race allow us."

"And what does that mean when it's got its spats on?"

"It means, milord, that we are not using our full team allowance." Blotto's expression suggested this didn't clarify matters much. "Apparently, according to the rules drawn up by Monsieur Jean-Marie Carré-Dagneau, each vehicle entered is allowed to have a complement of one Principal Driver . . ."

"Not wishing to take the icing off your birthday cake, Corky, I'm afraid that's me."

"I never thought otherwise, milord. But, as well as the Principal Driver, the regulations allow for two people who are referred to as 'mechanics'."

"Two?"

"Yes, milord."

"Two, not one."

"No, milord."

"So that means we could have another boddo along in the Lag with us."

"You are always very quick to pick up the pertinence of such ideas, milord."

"Oh, Corky, don't talk such guff. Anyway, it's a good ticket to know we could take on another greengage. But we don't really need one, do we?"

"Don't we, milord?"

"No, I'd have thought you and I were up to whatever slings and arrows — to quote Tennyson — the Great Road Race chucks at us."

"I am not so sure, milord."

"Come on, Corky, you're a whale on the internal combustion engine. You don't need some other pimply oik to teach you your business. Besides, surely, weight of another boddo's going to slow the Lag down, isn't it?"

"Not sufficiently to affect the outcome of the race, milord."

"You're jiggling my kneecap."

"No, absolutely serious, milord. I think we should take on an extra mechanic."

"But, in the name of strawberries, why?"

"Because, milord, if all the other entrants in the race have two mechanics, we might be at risk."

"'At risk'? What in the bobbles do you mean by that?"

Corky Froggett's red face grew grim. "As I found out during our latest dust-up with the sausage-stuffers, milord, two against three are not good odds."

"But, Corky, that was war. I think different rules apply in a Great Road Race."

"I wouldn't be so sure of that, milord," said the chauffeur darkly. "Not when there's foreigners involved. I think we should engage a second mechanic."

"If you say so. You're the expert on petrol-pumpers, Corky. It's going to take some doing, though, to find some suitable oil-swiveller before tomorrow."

"Don't worry, milord. I have already found one."

"And this is the prize!" From his lectern, Jean-Marie Carré-Dagneau indicated the huge chest on the table in front of him. "Inside it are ten thousand English sovereigns, coming from the days when money was money, made of gold . . . not just pieces of paper as it is

35

in these unromantic times . . . And within a few days, somebody who is present in this room tonight will be the proud possessor of this valuable chest . . . and its contents!"

Blotto wished the motor magnate would stop going on about the money. That wasn't the important thing about the Great Road Race. What really mattered was that the contest should be conducted according to the honourable precepts of gentlemanly behaviour. And that the best man won. Even as he had the thought, he mentally corrected himself. It wasn't the best man who would win. It was the best car, with some reasonably competent boddo inside it. And that car, he knew, would be his Lagonda. With customary self-deprecation, he reckoned that his own contribution would be minimal. He would just have the good fortune to be behind the wheel of an engineering miracle.

Finally seeing Jean-Marie Carré-Dagneau in the flesh, Blotto could not pretend to be very impressed. There was something about the man which was unavoidably . . . French. A certain foppishness, a way of using his hands in far too many fluttery feminine gestures. Still, what could you expect from a boddo half of whose first name was "Marie"?

"Now," Carré-Dagneau went on, "some of you may be asking why I, as a manufacturer of automobiles in France, should be offering a prize in English sovereigns rather than French francs. And there is a very simple answer to that question. It is that the family of

Carré-Dagneau is a very historic one in La France. We are aristocrats."

Hardly, thought Blotto. You're French. Even before the Revolution, an aristocratic title in France was about equivalent in rank to an English town councillor.

"The Carré-Dagneaux, therefore, are *royalistes*. And since in *La Belle France* — *quel dommage* — we do not have a monarch, I prefer to give, as prize money, coins which bear a King's head!"

Entirely reasonable, thought Blotto. No foreign money was ever going to be as reliable as the good old English pound. But he was still amused that a car salesman should be claiming aristocratic ancestry. One had only to look at Jean-Marie Carré-Dagneau to realise how far he was from the genuine article. True, he was wearing appropriate white tie and tails, but the patrician image was ruined by a diagonal red sash draped across his waistcoat, on which, in white letters, were embroidered the words: Les Automobiles Carré-Dagneau. That alone put him way beyond the barbed wire. Nobody with breeding would ever go around dressed as a billboard.

Blotto couldn't fault the Frenchman's choice of venue for the Sunday eve-of-race dinner, though. Drinks in one of the elegant river-facing rooms and then to the larger one next door for the meal. Blotto knew you could always trust the Savoy. In fact, when he was in London with Twinks, the pair of them always parked their pyjams at the Sawers. And, knowing the hotel's wine list off by heart, Blotto was also impressed by the champagne which Carré-Dagneau had selected for the pre-prandial drinks. No, the man did have a few things to commend him ... in spite of being a car salesman.

Blotto looked across at the other members of the Carré-Dagneau family. The wife, Adélaïde, was a large woman seated on a rather fragile-looking gold chair, and just about held in by an over-elaborate dress of white with gold trimmings. Her hairstyle, the result of painstaking topiary, resembled nothing so much as a dead squirrel. And she wore far more jewellery than anyone with genuine pretentions to the aristocracy would have done. As if being foreign wasn't bad enough, he reflected, she was vulgar too.

Next to her sat what could only be the precious son, Florian. Already predisposed not to like the young man, Blotto found the reality confirmed his prejudices. Florian Carré-Dagneau probably imagined he was wearing evening dress, but he was very far off the mark. For a start, his tailcoat was not black, but blue. Blue! Blotto was glad his sister wasn't there to witness this breach of decorum.

Then, to compound the felony, the young French-man was wearing a soft shirt! The kind of shirt that might just be acceptable on the cricket pitch, but had no place at the Savoy. Blotto and his Eton muffin-toasters had learnt from an early age the importance at social occasions of being acutely uncomfortable. If, at a formal dance, your shirt front didn't feel like a washboard, and your detached starched collar wasn't sawing into your neck in at least three places, then you knew you had done something wrong.

Added to these two offences against propriety, Florian Carré-Dagneau also boasted a moustache! Now, Blotto himself had never indulged in facial hair, except when kept from his razor by kidnappers and other desperados, but he did know that there was a place for such adornment. Some people were incomplete with no facial hair. Corky Froggett, for example, would not have been Corky Froggett without his moustache, each individual bristle of which stood at permanent attention, as if anticipating inspection by its commanding officer.

But Corky could grow a moustache. His had the robust quality of a kitchen implement designed to scour roasting trays. Whereas the thin residue of hair on the upper lip of Florian Carré-Dagneau did not look up to the task of polishing glassware. It was just a smudge, as though he had made too impetuous an approach to a chocolate ice cream. Taken in combination with his more or less total lack of chin, it made the young man look effete and . . . well, irredeemably French.

Blotto had not started out with much anxiety about the challenge from the man Florian in the car Florian, but now, having seen what he was up against, he knew that he and the Lag would soon be rolling on camomile lawns.

Next to the Carré-Dagneau boy sat a sulky-looking girl of perhaps nineteen. With a different facial expression, she might have been beautiful. At that moment, however, she looked as though she'd just realised that the lemon she had bitten into contained half a live maggot. She was dressed in the style of a wedding cake and looked enough like Adélaïde Carré-Dagneau to suggest that she must be Florian's sister. She had a fine voluptuous figure, which would no doubt in time go the way of her mother's, but hadn't yet.

Blotto looked around the room to check out the rest of the opposition, whose names were listed in the elaborately printed and tasselled programme which had been produced for the event. Again, the Carré-Dagneau company had not spared any expense. Of course, Blotto knew Trumbo McCorquodash and the rest of his Eton muffin-toasters. All excellent boddoes, the kind you'd be happy to go into the jungle with, and skilled racing drivers. But Blotto felt quietly confident that he and the Lagonda would have the jump on the lot of them.

He was more interested in the foreign contingent. The German driver probably looked the most daunting. Count Daspoontz had a shaven head. He wore a moustache, a monocle and an expression of utter contempt for everything his eye lighted upon. Standing at his shoulders were two men in dark uniforms, whose military demeanour made Corky Froggett's fingers itch to get hold of a Vickers machine-gun.

Though of humble rank, the chauffeur had been invited to the pre-prandial drinks and dinner because of his status as a mechanic in the Great Road Race. The engineers supporting the other drivers were also present, in each case two per car. In accordance with their station, few wore evening dress. Most were dressed in chauffeurs' uniforms or spotless overalls. Blotto wondered idly if Corky had thought any further about getting a second mechanic for the Lagonda, though he felt supremely confident of winning with just the two of them.

Corky, he could tell, was nervous. It had taken a lot of persuasion to get him to attend the reception. He felt his duty lay downstairs in the Savoy garage, protecting the spotless Lagonda from the vandals of whom, he felt certain, London was full. Blotto had virtually had to order him to come along.

His gaze shifted to the next threesome, whose very un-British gesticulations marked them out as the team from Italy. Their driver he identified from the programme as Enrico Parmigiano-Reggiano. Though in immaculate evening dress, the Fettuccine roadster driver wore a foppish blue velvet cap with a black tassel hanging from it. Blotto bridled at the sight. Great Wilberforce, tassels were decorations for women's garments, not men's! And people of breeding did not wear hats in the Savoy.

Parmigiano-Reggiano's mechanics were two swarthy thugs whose very appearance made Blotto check that his wallet was where he usually kept it.

He turned his attention to the American entry. For no reason that he could explain, there were seven of them, rather than three. All were wearing evening dress, presumably some expression of that egalitarianism which the Yanks so frequently talked about and so rarely put into practice. The driver, identified from the programme as Brad Gimlet, had the kind of blond hair, blue eyes, deeply tanned skin and gleaming teeth which might offer him Hollywood career opportunities if the frequent promise of colour in the movies ever came to fruition. He would be competing in the latest Cadebaker Cabriolet.

"Now, I wish to fill in a few more details," continued Jean-Marie Carré-Dagneau, still very gratified by the sound of his own voice. "*Les règles du jeu* . . . the rules of the game. We, the French, have always been famous for playing by the rules."

I'll take that with a dose of bicarb, thought Blotto.

"And so the Great Road Race will of course have rules. Twenty-five cars have been entered for the contest, and each has a team of one driver and two mechanics." Blotto didn't think it was the moment to correct Carré-Dagneau. He would wait to receive the plaudits when just the two of them, he and Corky, had won the race.

"The route," the automobile magnate went on, "will be divided into four sections — and, incidentally, how you make your route between the checkpoints is up to you and your navigators. The first section is from tomorrow's starting point in Trafalgar Square — where all vehicles will leave at two o'clock in the afternoon — to the ferry port at Dover.

"Now I am sure, when the idea of this Great Road Race came up, you were all asking yourselves how your automobiles would cross the English Channel to Calais. Each one on a small boat of its own, perhaps?" He chuckled at the incongruity of the idea. "But no. We at

Les Automobiles Carré-Dagneau are not only at the cutting edge of the technology of the motor car, we are also involved in the development of the latest sea-going transport. As I am sure you all know by now, your transport to *la belle France* will be in the brand-new Carré-Dagneau car ferry — called the *Jean-Marie*, as it happens. Your vehicles will be lifted by crane at the Port of Dover on to the deck of the vessel and lifted off by crane at the Port of Calais. And then you will continue the Great Road Race!"

The description of this advanced technology prompted whistles and cheers of admiration. Jean-Marie Carré-Dagneau smiled complacently, as he went on, "The next leg of your journey is from Calais, leaving at eight o'clock in the morning, and driving to the Carré-Dagneau family seat near Dijon, the Château d'Igeaux, where you will all spend the night as our guests. The third day's drive is from our Château to Monaco, where the third night will be spent in the Hôtel Huge. During the first three legs of the race, the driving may be shared amongst your team. But on the final leg the driver must be the nominated driver, the team captain. And that fourth leg of the Great Road Race will take you from Monaco to the finishing line, which is of course the Colosseum in Rome!"

The name of their destination was greeted by ebullient cheers from the assembled competitors.

"The times of the individual drivers will be recorded at the end of each leg, using the latest Swiss stopwatch technology. All automobiles will leave at eight o'clock each morning, and their arrival time will be noted each evening. At the ferry port in Dover, the relevant time will be the moment the car's wheels touch the deck after being craned aboard. At the Château d'Igeaux it will be as the vehicles pass through the gates, and so on.

"To ensure fair play, the person in charge of the time-keeping will be my lady wife, Madame Adélaïde Carré-Dagneau." He inclined his head towards her and received a gracious nod in return.

"Now the more intelligent among you . . ." Blotto stopped listening. He knew his limitations ". . . may be wondering how it is that Madame Carré-Dagneau will be in a position to do the time-keeping when she will need to be in place ahead of the fastest automobiles ever made. There is a simple answer to this question. Les Automobiles Carré-Dagneau not only produce the finest cars in the world . . ." In spite of the light-hearted way in which he spoke these words, they were greeted by a rumble of dissent. ". . . and the finest ferries to cross *La Manche*. We are also at the forefront of aeroplane manufacture.

"Madame and I will be making our way between the overnight stopping places in the latest, technologically advanced product of our aviation factories, the Carré-Dagneau cargo plane. This is the most efficient aircraft yet produced for the transportation of heavy loads of freight. But it can also, with the minimum disruption, be converted back into a passenger plane. This miracle of modern engineering is called the Giselle — named, of course, after my beautiful daughter." The young woman referred to looked sulkier

44

than ever. "And our travelling by this wonderful aeroplane will ensure that my wife is always at her time-keeping post long before the first of the competing vehicles arrive.

"The system on which the timing will be based is very simple. Madame Carré-Dagneau's stopwatch will be clicked on at the sound of the starting signal each morning, and she will note the arrival time at the day's destination of each vehicle. The accumulated times will be added up and, when the Great Road Race reaches its climax at the Colosseum in Rome, the chest of gold sovereigns will be awarded to the team with the shortest overall time . . . which may of course also be the team in the first car to pass the chequered flag."

Jean-Marie Carré-Dagneau raised his champagne glass. "So, I wish good luck to everyone involved and — as you say rather quaintly in this old-fashioned country — may the best man win!"

Blotto thought that was fair. Though brought up from an early age to resist the mortal sin of "showing off", in the current circumstances he knew himself to be the best man.

It soon became clear, however, that he wasn't the only person in the room of that opinion. In the mêlée at the end of Jean-Marie Carré-Dagneau's speech, as the champagne glasses were generously refilled, Blotto found himself approached by a gaggle of the other drivers.

"Hi, I'm Brad Gimlet," said the American, proffering his hand and revealing some yards of white teeth. "You must be Devereux Lyminster."

"Yes, that's the label on the programme, but everyone calls me Blotto."

"Then hi there, Blotto. Well, everyone I talk to tells me you're the man to beat."

"Oh, don't talk such toffee," came the instinctive response. He'd never been good at taking compliments.

"Ah, but it is true," said Florian Carré-Dagneau, whose voice turned out to be as droopy as his moustache. "You are ... how you say, the 'ot favourite."

"You're talking through your elbow patch," said Blotto modestly.

"Nein, zis iz vot all ze volk are saying," Count Daspoontz asserted, his two uniformed heavies still at his shoulders.

"It's true," Enrico Parmigiano-Reggiano contributed. "Everyone tells me my Fettuccine roadster will be no match for your Lagonda."

"Oh, puddledash! I have just the same chances as all the rest of you boddoes."

The Italian shook his head. "That's not what the bookmakers are saying."

"'Bookmakers'? By Denzil, are you telling me some greengages out there are actually putting money on this shooting match?"

"A great deal of money, Blotto. And you, let me tell you, are at very short odds."

"So be very careful," advised Florian Carré-Dagneau, in a voice of silken menace. "There are a lot of people who would like to see you don't make it to the starting grid tomorrow."

"Oh, now you're talking pure meringue," said Blotto. "I have to remind all of you poor thimbles that you're in England now, and in England there are certain codes we abide by. Nobody's going to play a diddler's hand in an event that starts in Trafalgar Square."

He might have said more, but he was interrupted by the banging of a gavel on Jean-Marie Carré-Dagneau's lectern. "And now," the motor manufacturer announced, "let us go through to the dining room to enjoy our dinner. To whet your appetites, may I tell you that the Savoy have agreed to let me bring my own chef from Château d'Igeaux, to provide you with a banquet of culinary delights. And tonight's menu starts with one of his signature recipes — a dish which has sent ripples through the world of fine dining — his very special Coquilles-St-Jacques!"

It wasn't just the world of fine dining through which the chef's Coquilles-St-Jacques had sent ripples, thought Blotto in anguish at three o'clock in the morning, as he had to make another rush to the bathroom, his eleventh that night.

CHAPTER
FIVE

The Second Mechanic

Not much sleeping was done that night, but Blotto was woken from an uneasy doze at eight o'clock the following morning by a call from Reception. Corky Froggett was put on the line, and he sounded as washed out as the Young Master felt.

"I think it may have been the scallops, milord," he gasped.

"Yes, seafood can be iffy," Blotto agreed. "Easily give a boddo the squiff-squits. I've had trouble with an oofy oyster before now. These things happen. Just tough Gorgonzola that it's happened the night before the Great Road Race."

"I think we ought to do some planning before the race starts, milord."

"Tickey-Tockey."

"Could you meet me down at Reception, milord?"

"Well, I could *try*." Blotto didn't sound convinced. Then, as another rush to the bathroom became imperative, he shouted out, "You'd better come up here!", and left the telephone receiver dangling from its wire.

★ ★ ★

It went against every instinct in Corky Froggett's peasant soul to use the facilities in the Young Master's suite, but gastric upsets have never shown much respect for protocol. As a result, employer and chauffeur boxed and coxed in and out of the bathroom for some hours. Eventually, drained (in every sense), Blotto laid feebly back on his bed, and Corky, incapable of standing in his superior's presence (as he normally had never failed to do), collapsed on to a *chaise longue*.

"This is a total candle-snuffer," moaned Blotto. "I'm as weak as a kitten with the crimps."

"I know what you mean, milord," groaned Corky. "I haven't felt so gammy since a bout of dysentery that I had on the Somme during the last little dust-up with the Hun. And the latrines in the trenches were not —"

"Rein in the roans there, Corky. I don't think we need the full chapter and versicle."

"Very good, milord." There was an awkward silence. Then the chauffeur went on, "I'm afraid I have to tell you, milord, that I have failed in my duty to you."

"How's that?"

"After the dinner yesterday evening, it had been my firm intention to go straight down to the hotel garage and keep vigil over the Lagonda all night. There are some nasty types in London, I know, and I would never have forgiven myself if any harm had come to my Young Master's car. However, before I could reach the garage, I was struck by the first attack of the gastric trouble which has kept me on the go ever since. Milord, I can never forgive myself."

"Don't don your worry-boots about that, Corky. If you felt half as crocked as I have all night, there's no way you could have made it down to the garage."

"Perhaps not, but I still feel that I've failed in my duty. If it is your view that my going into the adjacent room with your old service revolver to 'do the decent thing' might help the situation, I'd be only too happy to —"

"There's no need. The two of us are as crocked as each other."

"Yes, milord."

"Fact is, Corky, I could no more drive the Lag today than I could score a century with one arm tied behind my back."

"But surely, milord, you *did* score a century in the Eton and Harrow match with one arm tied behind your back in your debut season in the First Eleven."

"Oh yes, you're right. That memory'd slipped out of the brainbox, Corky. So not a very good example. But it just goes to show how spoffing diluted I am. Put me in a boxing ring right now with a piece of tissue paper, and the tissue paper'd win by a knockout in the first round."

"If you can't drive, milord, then I'm sure I can." The chauffeur boldly tried to rise from his *chaise longue* but collapsed back in a shapeless heap. Blotto observed that the man's face was as white as his moustache.

"No two ways about it, Corky. We're adrift in the same dinghy. Neither of us is up to driving a tiny's tricycle, let alone the Lag. We'll have to scratch from the starting lineup for the Great Road Race."

50

"But we can't do that, milord," the chauffeur responded instinctively.

"Then do you have any other way out of the whiffhole?"

Corky's silence was more eloquent than any words would have been.

"Oh, broken biscuits," said Blotto. The use of such strong language in the company of an inferior demonstrated the depth of his despair. "We're both feet in the quagmire, and no mistake. Oh, it's at times like this I wish Twinks was on the roll call. I'm sure she'd have some pill or potion in her sequinned reticule that'd sort out our gut-gripes. And if she bent her brainbox to the problem, she'd find a way of getting the Lag on to the starting grid."

"Might it not be possible," suggested Corky Froggett weakly, "to telephone her ladyship and ask her to come to our assistance?"

"No pay-out there, I'm afraid, Corky. Twinks is off in the tartan wilds of Scotland, trying to snare a husband and learn about water colours."

Corky looked puzzled. "But water doesn't have any colour, does it?" he asked, reasonably enough. "That's the most important thing about water."

Blotto didn't have the energy to offer any kind of explanation. The two men lay in silence, prostrated by calamity in the form of Coquilles-St-Jacques.

Then there was a knock at the door.

"Come in," Blotto called out in a frail voice.

There entered into his suite a slight young man dressed in one-piece white leather overalls. He had strikingly blue eyes, and his hair was hidden under a white leather aviator's cap, on to the brow of which white-framed goggles had been pushed up. Hanging from his belt was a white leather satchel.

"Hi," he said, in a rather high-pitched American accent. "I understand you guys might be looking for a second mechanic."

"Not on your nuthatch!" Blotto responded instinctively. "We can see the sword home with just the two of us."

"Oh yes?" The mechanic looked pityingly down at the enfeebled pair. "Neither of you has enough puff to turn a toy windmill. The scallops in that Cocky-Saint-Jakes, was it?" he suggested.

"That's the way the likelihood's leaning," groaned Blotto. "Are you part of the American line-up?"

"Sure was," replied the young man. "We came over with six mechanics."

"Yanks always have a tendency to over-cater," Blotto observed. "They like everything big. Like the size of the meals they serve up in their restaurants."

"Yeah, well, we get here and find that each team's only allowed two mechanics, so I'm bounced outta the party. And then, when this gentleman —" he gestured towards the horizontal chauffeur — "said you might be looking for a second mechanic, I jumped at the chance."

Blotto looked reproachfully at Corky. "You know I told you we could come up with the silverware, just the two of us."

"Indeed I do, milord. And I was planning to consult you about the matter, but sadly . . ." He clutched at his stomach ". . . other imperatives took over."

52

"You're bong on the nose there," said Blotto, clutching his own stomach in sympathy. "I say, a thought's just boffed me on the bonce." This was a rare enough occurrence to engage Corky Froggett's full attention, as his master turned back to the young mechanic. "Tell me, did any of your American team get struck down with the gut-gripes?"

"No, sir."

He looked at Corky. "Then it can't have been the scallops, can it?"

Before the chauffeur could respond, the mechanic said, "Don't be so sure of that, sir. None of our team ate the food they were served up with in the dining room last night. Our Fitness Director has put us all on special diets. So, we bring our own food."

"'Fitness Director'?" Blotto echoed contemptuously. "What's a 'Fitness Director' when he's got his spats on?"

"He's the guy who dictates our diet and exercise regime. Kinda oversees our training."

"'Training'?" This didn't sound any better to Blotto. It carried with it the nasty whiff of "practising", that close relative of cheating, to which the Americans were so prone. As a race, the Yanks could never understand the fine British tradition of "the gifted amateur". They didn't understand that sporting prowess should be innate and instinctive.

"Anyway," the young mechanic went on, "back in North Carolina, where I come from, we have an old saying: 'The tree's gonna fall somewhere, just make sure you're not the one underneath it'."

53

"Good ticket," said Blotto. Then, after a silence, "And what, in the name of Wilberforce, does that mean?"

"It means, sir, that, because we had taken appropriate precautions, none of our team got nobbled by the poisoned scallops."

'Poisoned'? Blotto found he was echoing the young man quite a lot. "Are you suggesting the scallops were poisoned?"

"Too right I am, sir."

"But what kind of four-faced filcher would want to poison a Coquilles-St-Jacques? At the Savoy, of all places? And, come to that, why would they do it?"

"Well, obviously, to weaken the opposition." Blotto looked thunderstruck. "The way I see it, sir, the Carré-Dagneau family are so determined to win this Great Road Race with their new Florian automobile that they will stop at nothing to attain their ends."

"The thimble-jigglers! Surely, they wouldn't have done that? Poisoning the Coquilles-St-Jacques? It's a blatant act of sabbatical."

" 'Sabotage', I think, is the word you're looking for, sir," suggested the mechanic.

"Quite possibly. Anyway, how does a young oil-monkey like you know all this gubbins? Were you at the dinner last night?"

"I sure was, sir. All the US team was there. So, I saw who ate the Cocky-Saint-Jakes and who didn't. And everyone who did eat them was struck down overnight with the runs."

" 'Runs'?" Yet another echo from Blotto. "I didn't know we were talking about cricket."

Corky Froggett helped him out. " 'The runs', sir, is a colloquial expression which refers to what the Quality call the gut-gripes."

"Oh, Tickey-Tockey. On the same page now." He turned back to the young American. "And you really think the Carré-Dagneaux set up the whole shooting match?"

"I'm sure they did, sir."

"The out-of-bounders!" said Blotto. "How could anyone be as four-faced as that?"

"They are French, milord," his chauffeur pointed out.

"Yes, Corky, but I mean, even so . . . I've met some lumps of toadspawn in my time, but to serve up poisoned scallops . . . and in the Savvers . . . well, that's way outside the rule book." Blotto always endeavoured to think the best of people, until the evidence of skulduggery was irrefutable. He turned back to the mechanic. "Are you sure you haven't got the wrong end of the sink-plunger, young sprig?"

"No, sir. I kept a very close eye on everything that happened at the dinner last night. I suspected there might be some under-the-counter work going on. Back in North Carolina, we have an old saying: 'The wise woodchuck is the woodchuck who watches the other woodchucks.'

Blotto looked bemused. "Weren't you on your guard too, sir, checking out what food you were served?"

"No, by Denzil! Not at the Sawers. There's never any trouble with what's put in the nosebags at the Sawers."

"You forget, milord," Corky Froggett interposed, "that last night's food wasn't prepared by the Savoy kitchens. That Carré-Dagneau squiffball had brought in his own chef."

"Toad-in-the-hole, you're right, Corky!"

"Who was, needless to say, French."

"What is more —" the mechanic picked up his cue — "it was very noticeable that some of the guests didn't touch the first course."

"The Coquilles-St-Jacques? Who didn't eat it?"

"None of the Carré-Dagneau family touched it. Not the boss, not his wife, not their daughter, and not their hornswoggler of a son."

"Toad-in-the-hole!"

"What's more, some of the English drivers, they didn't touch it either."

"Which English drivers?"

"The ones who brayed."

"'Brayed'?" This echoing the American mechanic was becoming a habit.

"I think, milord, the young gentleman is referring to your schoolfriends . . ."

"Oh, Tickey-Tockey."

"You don't think they were part of the conspiracy too, milord, do you?"

"Corky, wash your mouth out with the old carbolic. You're talking about chaps from Eton."

"I beg your pardon, milord. But very few of them ate —"

Blotto overrode him. "The reason my old muffin-toasters didn't eat the Coquilles-St-Jacques was just they don't like frenchified food. I mean, they would have eaten the second course, the steak . . . once they'd wiped the sauce off it, obviously. But anything outside meat and two veg or rice pudding is a bit beyond the barbed wire for those boddoes." Blotto clutched at his once again griping stomach. "Mind you, now I wish I'd been like them and laid off the first course gubbins."

"So, why didn't you, milord?"

"The Mater — and a whole regiment of nannies — always dinned into me that I should leave a nice clean plate! Never escape those things you're taught in the nursery. But, come to that, Corky, why did you eat the Coquilles-St-Jacques?"

The palest of blushes sidled across the chauffeur's white face. "I'm afraid, milord, that, while I was spending time with . . . a certain French person, I did develop a taste for the cooking of her country."

"Ah. On the same page." Blotto did not press further. He recalled the chauffeur's liaison with the couturier Madame Clothilde of Mayfair, first met in wartime France under her real name Yvette. Their rekindled romance in London had ended unhappily, and Blotto knew better than to intrude into another boddo's private grief.

He turned back to the mechanic. "Did your peepers pinpoint anyone else who didn't touch the Coquilles?"

"Yes, sir. Neither the German team nor the Italians went near them."

"Hm. Do you think that was just a pride flipmadoodle? You know, thinking their own home cooking was a better boffo than anything the garlic-guzzlers could come up with?"

"It could be that, sir," the boy conceded politely, "but I think it's more likely they were warned off."

"By whom? Surely those Carré-Dagneau lumps of toadspawn wouldn't tell them?"

"No, sir. But I'm sure both the German and Italian teams have spies in the Carré-Dagneau camp. I know we Yanks do."

Blotto looked bewildered as he produced yet another echo. " 'Spies'? Everyone seems to be taking this whole clangdumble a bit seriously, don't they? It's just a Road Race, after all. An opportunity for a bunch of gentlemen to get together and see who's got the fastest car. Why, in the name of strawberries, should that get people to start using spies?"

"You may be forgetting, sir, that there are ten thousand gold sovereigns at stake."

"Yes, I suppose that might add a trumpet to the trombone." Blotto looked disconsolately across at the evacuated Corky. "So, it was just us two got booby-trapped, was it?"

"A few other minor players are out of commission this morning, sir. But you're the only ones of the main players. The starting line-up is now down to fourteen cars."

"Does that include us, me lad?" asked Corky.

"It'll be fifteen, if you make it."

"Well, of course we'll make it!" said Blotto.

"Of course, we will, milord!" said Corky Froggett.

Valiantly, both men rose from their recumbent positions. Both stood up. Both immediately fell back down again.

"I'm afraid, sir, neither of you are in any condition to do anything."

"No," Blotto agreed gloomily. "Broken biscuits! Oh, I wish my sister Twinks was here. She can always find her way out of the deepest gluepot. I mean, if she were here now, she'd produce out of her sequinned reticule some pill or potion that'd get us ready to tame a lion in no time."

"Well . . . Back in North Carolina, we have an old saying: 'What you can't see isn't there.' " The American mechanic looked around the suite. "I'm afraid I don't see any sign of the young lady."

"No, more's the moping . . ."

"On the other hand," the boy went on, "I do happen to have in my leather satchel some pills and potions." He reached and produced a small sequinned pillbox. "These are based on traditional herbal remedies created by Cherokee medicine men, who used to roam the plains of North Carolina, where I come from." He opened the box and extracted four round pink pills. Handing two to each man, he said, "Take these. You'll be able to swallow them down without water."

Both were too reduced to ask what they were ingesting. They gulped down the pills.

"Now, these'll make you start to feel better immediately, but you'll need to drink a lot of water to replace the fluid you've lost. It'll take a few hours for you to get your strength back."

"How many hours?"

"Around six."

Blotto looked at his bedside clock and groaned. "That's too spoffing long. It's now eleven o'clock and the Great Road Race bully-off is at two. Is there any chance we'll feel tweaked up for driving in less than six hours?"

"No chance at all, sir. In fact, the Cherokee chief Stamping-My-Little-Foot Eagle once took some of these for a stomach upset and made the mistake of attacking a Waccamaw war party four hours later. His entire party was killed and scalped. If he'd only waited two more hours, he would have blown the Waccamaws away, and the whole history of America would have been different."

"Oh, rodents!" said Blotto. "We're going to have to scratch. If neither of us can hold the steering wheel."

"Oh . . ." Corky Froggett had been about to use a stronger expression but, remembering he was in the Young Master's presence, made do with: "Bother!"

"There is one other possibility," the American mechanic suggested diffidently.

"What?" groaned Blotto. "I'd accept anything that got my boots out of the bilges."

"Back in North Carolina, we have a saying: 'If there's only one pot in your kitchen, that's the one you're going to use.'" Seeing Blotto's blankness, he explained, "If you made me your second mechanic, I could drive the car."

60

"You? Have you any experience of driving a Lagonda?"

"My training covered the driving of all cars currently on the road, not only in the States, but all over the world."

"Hmm . . ." Blotto thought about the idea. This was always a slow process.

Corky Froggett had a more basic concern. "Erm . . . During the six hours of our . . . erm, recuperation, will we still be having to . . . erm, make use of the facilities with such frequency? I was thinking that might rather slow down our progress in the Great Road Race."

"No worries," said the youth. "The pills will have already dealt with that phase of your recovery. No, for the next six hours you will sleep, and then wake up factory-fresh, ready for any challenge that life may throw at you."

"Splendid," said Corky, slumping back on to the *chaise longue* and falling instantly asleep.

"Good ticket," murmured Blotto drowsily. "So, look, you will wake us up to pongle over to Trafalgar Square for the start."

"I guarantee I'll get both of you safely there, sir."

"You're a good greengage. What's your name?"

"My name is Ronald, sir."

"Ronald," Blotto mumbled. "People call me 'Blotto'."

"I know that, sir."

"Ronald," he repeated. "That's a good name."

"Thank you, sir."

Then, just before sleep claimed him, Blotto looked closely at the young man. "Haven't I seen you somewhere before?"

"I don't know, sir. Have you ever been to Boogersville, North Carolina?"

"Great Wilberforce, no!"

"Then I don't think you will have seen me before, sir," said Ronald the Second Mechanic.

CHAPTER
SIX

They're Off!

Whatever the Cherokee medicine man had put into his pink pills, they certainly did the business. Blotto and Corky were entirely comatose while the Second Mechanic packed the former's luggage and went to the downmarket hotel where the latter had been billeted to pick up his bags.

He then somnambulated the two men down to the Savoy garage and got them installed in the Lagonda, Corky slumped in the back, and Blotto stretched out in the passenger seat. Within minutes, they were once again dead to the world. Ronald the Second Mechanic stowed the luggage in the boot. And stowed some very special items in the car's capacious, but hidden, under-chassis compartments. He also attached special devices to the back of the car, beneath the dickey. In all of these actions, he was preparing for any eventuality. In fact, he was following the principle expressed in the old saying from North Carolina: "The man who carries five umbrellas never gets wet."

Then he drove sedately from the Savoy to Trafalgar Square.

No expense had been spared for the start of the Great Road Race. Hiring such an iconic tourist destination cannot have been either easy or cheap. And it might have been wondered whether the London civic authority which gave permission for the usage had anticipated the number of flags on the scene promoting the products of Les Automobiles Carré-Dagneau. They might have expected to see the red and white pennants attached to the competing cars, but surely they had not been consulted about the huge red ribbon, printed with the manufacturer's name in white, which wound its spiral way down from the top of Nelson's Column to the bottom. But then, from the Revolution onward, the French have always been fond of flags. As a nation, they feel bereft if they haven't got something to wave from a barricade.

The French have also always been fond, thought Ronald the Second Mechanic as he looked at the other competing vehicles on the grid, of ghastly colours. The Carré-Dagneau Florian was violet, for the love of strawberries! Violet! That was no colour for a car. It might be acceptable in the dress of a rather flighty woman with a dubious past, but never in a car. The colour choice just added another to the long list of inadequacies of the French.

The Carré-Dagneau publicity machine had also been very effective in bringing out the press to Trafalgar Square. Reporters, notebooks at the ready, clustered round the drivers. Magnesium flared as photographers recorded the scene. Huge movie cameras on tripods were cranked by busy operatives making newsreels.

Soon all Europe — if not the entire world — would know that the Great Road Race was happening.

When the Lagonda arrived on the starting grid, it too was surrounded by reporters, eager to talk to Devereux Lyminster, the race favourite. The fact that he and his First Mechanic were asleep could not be hidden, but the car's young leather-clad driver coolly insisted that this was part of their race strategy. He would undertake the driving through the outskirts of London and, once they were in the open country, a refreshed and re-energised Devereux Lyminster would take the wheel. The reporters were impressed by these novel tactics. Clearly, the English were beginning to learn from the Americans in the unsavoury business of training for sporting events.

During the build-up to the actual start, Ronald the Second Mechanic kept a shrewd eye on the other competitors, keen to see who expressed surprise at the Lagonda's arrival. Anyone who did would obviously become a suspect for the crime of Blotto- and Corky-knobbling by means of dodgy scallops.

But the people he was dealing with were far too canny operators to give themselves away that easily. Many of the Principal Drivers — Florian Carré-Dagneau, Enrico Parmigiano-Reggiano and Count Daspoontz — came up to the car to wish the British team good luck, but none behaved in a suspicious manner, or commented on the unconscious bodies in the back. They just indulged in the light-hearted banter that might be expected from fellow competitors approaching a major test of their skill.

Brad Gimlet was one of the last to approach the Lagonda and express his good wishes. He showed no signs of recognising the driver as a refugee from his own team. But then why should he? None of his other mechanics were wearing white leather overalls. He returned to his huge Cadebaker Cabriolet to ready himself for the challenge ahead.

All of the competitors had been advised of the arrangements for the start of the Great Road Race. The area around Trafalgar Square and the whole length of The Mall had been closed to other traffic between one o'clock and two thirty (it must have cost a fortune to get the police and civic authorities to agree to that). By one thirty, the remaining fifteen competing cars had to be lined up across Trafalgar Square, in an order determined by ballot. They would be facing the new Admiralty Arch, which Edward VII had commissioned as a memorial to his late mother, Queen Victoria, but sadly did not survive to see completed.

All of the driving teams had to be in their vehicles by one forty-five. They were permitted to have their engines running before the off (because they were state-of-the-art vehicles, all had self-starters). The cue for the race to get under way would be the second bong of Big Ben striking two. Because of potential difficulties raised by traffic noise and wind direction, the sound would be relayed from the Houses of Parliament to Trafalgar Square by the latest, horrendously expensive, loudspeaker technology.

Once the race was up and running, the Carré-Dagneau family would be whisked, by a fast car of their own manufacture (which happened to be called the "Adélaïde"), to Croydon Aerodrome. They would be flown thence, in their Carré-Dagneau Giselle, to an airstrip near Dover, so that Madame Adélaïde Carré-Dagneau would be at her station on the ferry long before the arrival of the leading car.

Dwarfed behind the steering wheel of the mighty Lagonda, Ronald the Second Mechanic looked at the task ahead and assessed his options. The Admiralty Arch in fact had three arches, opening out from Trafalgar Square on to The Mall, which ran straight down to Buckingham Palace. By established protocol, the central arch could only be used by members of the Royal Family. Recognising that the cosmopolitan competitors in the Great Road Race might not bother about such niceties, the authorities had enforced their rules by locking the gates on the central arch.

Ronald the Second Mechanic knew that the Lagonda would have the jump on all of the other English cars and their Old Etonian drivers. He also knew that long habit of driving on the wrong side of the road would make most of the foreign competitors aim for the right-hand archway. He was therefore determined to ensure that the Lagonda would be first into The Mall through the left-hand one. He then calculated that he could stay ahead of the pack all the way to Dover. And Blotto would be sufficiently recovered by the following morning to bring his superior skills to the driving on the other side of the Channel.

The first part of the plan worked beautifully. Though the air was heavy with the sounds of revving engines, the amplified tones of Big Ben could be heard to perfection. The introductory chimes rang out across the openness of Trafalgar Square, preparing the competitors for the off.

Then the first bong sounded. Instantly Enrico Parmigiano-Reggiano's Fettuccine roadster shot off the grid. Typical of the four-faced filchers, thought Ronald the Second Mechanic. You wouldn't expect pasta-poppers like that to understand the meaning of the word "rules".

He waited until the reverberation of the second bong ended and then unleashed the Lagonda's power. As he had anticipated, the Fettuccine roadster had made straight for the right-hand arch, but Ronald the Second Mechanic had overhauled the car before it got there. The Lagonda entered The Mall ahead of its rival, and by the time it passed Buckingham Palace, there were a hundred yards of daylight between the two vehicles.

Ronald the Second Mechanic pressed down on the accelerator, confident of increasing the distance between himself and the pursuers, confident also that the ten-thousand-pound prize was in the bag.

Though a system of road numbering had recently been introduced, it was by no means foolproof, and signposting throughout the British Isles remained erratic. So, Ronald the Second Mechanic did not put his trust in road signs. He had made detailed preparations, poring over maps in the days before the Great Road Race started, and memorised the list of villages and towns through which the Lagonda would speed on its way to Dover.

Ronald the Second Mechanic was enjoying the drive. His two passengers were still dead to the world, but he knew that both would be revived and fresh as daisies for the race's second leg in the morning. He had not seen any sign of another competitor since he left the Fettuccine roadster in his wake at Buckingham Palace, and had no doubts he would arrive at Adélaïde Carré-Dagneau's checkpoint on the ferry way ahead of the pack. He felt exhilarated. He almost found himself shouting out "Larksissimo!", but reminded himself that it was not an expression that would have much currency in Boogersville, North Carolina.

To compound his joy, the Lagonda swept past a sign that told him he had arrived on the outskirts of Dover.

At that point, there was a puttering sound from the mighty engine, and the car stopped.

CHAPTER
SEVEN

Out of One Gluepot . . .

Blotto and Corky Froggett were still sleeping so peacefully that Ronald the Second Mechanic felt it would be unfair to wake them. Anyway, as someone who had grown up self-reliant, he was determined to make his own way out of the current mess.

By now it was dark. He got out of the car and extracted an electric torch from the white leather satchel at his waist. Before loosing the leather straps that held down the Lagonda's mighty bonnet to investigate major mechanical failures, he lay underneath the behemoth to check the underside of the chassis.

It wasn't subtle, but it had been effective. Silver glinted from the edge of the fresh hole that had been drilled in the bottom of the fuel tank. There was a strong smell of petrol from where the last of it had drained out. The detail wasn't important now, but Ronald the Second Mechanic wondered when the sabotage had been effected. Probably in the Savoy garage the previous night while Corky's vigilance had been compromised by the dodgy Coquilles-St-Jacques. But, if that were the case, why hadn't he noticed the fuel drained out on to the garage floor? He reckoned some kind of temporary bung must have been inserted, something that would stay in place on a level surface but be shaken out by the bumpy roadways of Kent.

And which of the rival drivers had been responsible for the sabotage? Or had it been done by one of the Carré-Dagneau family? Increasingly, Ronald the Second Mechanic was coming round to the idea that the sole purpose of the Great Road Race was to promote the new Florian automobile, and its manufacturers would resort to any skulduggery to ensure that their car won.

Anyway, such speculation could be kept for later. His current priority was to get the Lagonda back on the road. Needless to say, he had the requisite repair tools in his white leather satchel. He deftly plugged the drilled hole in the fuel tank with a specially designed bung which would spread on the inside to form a permanent seal.

There were spare cans of petrol in the Lagonda's boot, but Ronald the Second Mechanic ignored them, and went instead to the secret compartment under the chassis. From that he extracted a funnel and a larger container, whose contents he decanted into the fuel tank.

Though Ronald the Second Mechanic worked with exemplary efficiency, the repair did inevitably take time. And he was annoyed to see the Lagonda's lead in the first leg of the Great Road Race slowly eroded. The first car to pass him was the Fettuccine roadster, its Les Automobiles Carré-Dagneau pennant streaming in the wind behind it. He hadn't expected the Italian team to have shown any sympathy for his predicament, but he could have done without Enrico Parmigiano-Reggiano's disgusting hand gesture and the ribald shouts from his mechanics.

The next vehicle to go past during the refuelling process was Brad Gimlet's Cadebaker. Though the Americans were not as directly offensive as the Italians, there was still an element of smug triumphalism in their cheery shouts and waves. And, again, none of them showed any sign of recognising their former team member.

Ronald the Second Mechanic was no more than irritated by the way his lead was being whittled away. He had complete confidence that, on the open roads of France, with Blotto at the wheel, the Lagonda would quickly make up its lost ground and knock the opposition into a cockleshell. Splendissimo, he thought to himself at the prospect, before remembering that such an expression was unusual in Boogersville, North Carolina.

The next car to swoosh past was the eight-litre Krumpfenbach of Count Daspoontz. His team's responses to the grounded Lagonda at the roadside were harsh Teutonic laughter and some very strange salutes.

Then Trumbo McCorquodash's Bentley thundered past. The top was open. Trumbo took up both the driver and passenger seats in the front. He drove casually with one hand on the steering wheel. In the other he held the neck of a magnum of champagne, from which he took frequent swigs. Behind him were two young cousins, both still at Eton, who were acting as mechanics for their older relative.

As the Bentley passed, Trumbo McCorquodash roared out, "Whose car's driving like a Mark IV tank now, Blotters me old backscratcher?" The cousins echoed his fruity hilarity.

It was with great relief that Ronald the Second Mechanic finished his refuelling, returned the empty can to its compartment, and got back into the driver's seat.

He looked again at his two passengers. Both were sleeping far more peacefully than any baby had ever done. He decided to let them sleep on until the Cherokee medicine man's remedy had completed its good work. Then the next morning the pair of them would be factory-fresh.

Just at the moment he pressed the self-starter, another car roared past him. The Carré-Dagneau Florian of Florian Carré-Dagneau! Ronald the Second Mechanic regretted that the Frenchman would get to the ferry before him, but it was only a mild annoyance. On the other side of the Channel, the Lagonda's power could not fail to triumph.

The great car responded beautifully to Ronald the Second Mechanic's touch as it roared ahead. If there had been any room to overtake on the narrow streets of Dover, it would undoubtedly have changed the order of arrival at the port but, there being no such opportunities, the Fettuccine roadster arrived beside the ferry first. Then came the Americans' Cadebaker Cabriolet, followed by Count Daspoontz's Krumpfenbach

Big Eight, Trumbo McCorquodash's Bentley, Florian's Florian, and finally the Lagonda.

As he waited at the dockside, Ronald the Second Mechanic wondered idly which of their rivals had organised the hole in his fuel tank. His list of suspects was headed by the Carré-Dagneau family. He wondered what further diddler's doing the French squiffballs were lining up for their rivals. And decided that, once on the ferry, he would maintain a continuous overnight vigil in the Lagonda to prevent any more attempts at sabotage.

He watched as first the Fettuccine roadster, then the Cadebaker and the Krumpfenbach were loaded laboriously on to a cradle and lifted by crane on to the ferry deck. Once they were *in situ*, while the crew strapped the cars down so that they would not shift during the voyage, the drivers were presumably checked in and had their times recorded by Adélaïde Carré-Dagneau with her Swiss stopwatch.

As he waited, other competitors drew up behind him. They were mostly cars driven by other Old Etonian friends of Blotto's. None of them caused the mechanic even a flicker of anxiety. Their schoolmate from Tawcester Towers had many times demonstrated his superiority over them in every form of sporting contest.

But Ronald the Second Mechanic was beginning to find the wait wearisome. And he reflected that the rules imposed by Jean-Marie Carré-Dagneau were not the most efficient way of timing the first leg of the Great Road Race. The times should have been taken when the competing cars arrived at the dock, not when their wheels touched the deck of the ferry. Each car's dimensions were different and the crane's cradle had to be adjusted accordingly. So, the timings were erratic and, though the order of arrival was unchanged, the time added on for the craning process varied wildly. The light Fettuccine roadster was hoisted and deposited on to the deck with no delay, but the huge juggernauts like the Cadebaker and the Krumpfenbach took much longer.

Ronald the Second Mechanic's first thought was that the proposed system was just inefficiency on the Carré-Dagneaux's part, but then he realised that — of course — it was part of their plan. Their own car, the Florian, was by far the lightest of all the entrants. Craning that on board the ferry would take no time at all. So, if the duration of the lifting process were added to his arrival time, Florian Carré-Dagneau, despite arriving at the dock in fifth place, might end up with a total time which put him first.

And the weight of the Lagonda would ensure that even more unwanted minutes were added to its own score.

Ronald the Second Mechanic watched in dismay as, proving his prediction correct, the Florian was picked up like a featherweight and deposited on the deck of the ferry in less than a minute. Getting the Krumpfenbach Big Eight on board had taken nearly ten.

The Carré-Dagneaux had rigged the whole race! Ronald the Second Mechanic was as strongly against the idea of cheating as Blotto himself. What other kind of sneaky backdoor-sidling might the four-faced French filchers be up to?

He got his answer very quickly. As soon as the Carré-Dagneau Florian had touched down and been strapped to the deck, all activity on the ferry seemed to be suspended. The crane moved back to its resting position. No attempt was made to fix the required harness around the Lagonda. Ronald the Second Mechanic checked the time on the watch he kept in his white leather satchel and saw that a full eight minutes had elapsed since the embarkation of the Florian. This was cheating on a gargantuan scale!

But worse was to come. Suddenly he was aware of shouted orders from the ferry, and the sight of sailors rushing to release the hawsers which held it to the Dover dockside.

The French lumps of toadspawn were going to leave the remaining competitors on the quay!

CHAPTER
EIGHT

Up, Up and Away!

The cars behind him in the queue were mostly driven by Old Etonians, all of whom got out on to the dockside and started braying out ferocious condemnation of the Carré-Dagneau family. Old international conflicts rose to mind. Crécy and Agincourt were mentioned, along with the blatant disrespect the French commoners had shown to their aristocracy during the Revolution. All right, they had only been French aristocrats and therefore not very important, but removing their heads was still way beyond the barbed wire. The consensus seemed to be that allowing the ferry to leave without all the competitors on board was characteristic behaviour from the stenchers who lived the other side of the Channel.

Ronald the Second Mechanic did not have time to listen to such guff. Speed was of the essence. How fortunate that he had stuck to the principle expressed in the old North Carolina saying about the man with five umbrellas. He had prepared for any eventuality, and the latest example of French perfidy was, of course, covered by his preparations.

It was a matter of seconds for him to open the Lagonda's secret compartment and take out the pair of ramps which he had secreted there. Less than a minute had elapsed before he had them joined together and fixed to the edge of the quay. He then backed the mighty car as far as there was space on the dockside, engaged a forward gear and pressed the accelerator down to the floor.

At that moment, he heard the triumphant blast of a foghorn from the ferry, as it slipped away from the Dover dockside.

Even if he'd wanted to, which he didn't, Ronald the Second Mechanic could not have stopped his vehicle's forward momentum. Its huge tyres engaged with the ramps (which had of course been exactly calibrated to match its wheel-span), and suddenly the Lagonda was airborne!

It was at that moment that Ronald the Second Mechanic decided to stop being Ronald the Second Mechanic. After all, the ramp technology had not been created in Boogersville, North Carolina. It was the result of many months of experimentation, of trial and error conducted in an empty stable at Tawcester Towers. And now that it had actually worked, its inventor and sole creator, Twinks, wanted to take all the credit for herself.

But this wasn't the moment for such diversionary thoughts. In the split second between her realising that the car wasn't going to make it and its inevitable crashing into the ferry's stern, Twinks activated the device which she'd attached to the back of the Lagonda in the Savoy garage.

Instantly, the booster rocket she had designed (following the research and techniques developed by Robert Esnault-Pelterie, Robert Goddard and Yves Le Prieur) ignited, raising the trajectory of the Lagonda, so that the huge vehicle just cleared the ferry's transom.

As soon as she made deckfall, Twinks activated the retrorocket, and slammed on the brakes.

The Lagonda came to a perfect halt in the space next to the Carré-Dagneau Florian. Blotto and Corky stirred in their seats but did not wake. The Cherokee medicine man's potion was doing its stuff.

All of the ferry's crew were busy below decks or at the fore of the vessel, and no one witnessed the Lagonda's dramatic arrival.

Twinks murmured to herself the single word, "Splendissimo!" She had countered yet another of the Carré-Dagneaux's acts of sabotage.

Onshore, the ramp was still in place, and one of Blotto's old muffin-toasters hastily backed his brand-new Riley Nine away from the dockside and roared forward to follow the Lagonda's trajectory. Sadly, although he hit the ramp perfectly, the ferry had by then moved too far away from land. An extremely angry and wet Old Etonian had to be rescued from his sunken vehicle by the Dover Coastguard.

Twinks noted the time her wheels had touched the deck, then got out of the car and punctiliously removed the booster and retro rockets, decanting their remains into the sea. Then she attached to the Lagonda the strapping that was in place to fix it to the deck, to prevent movement in choppy waters.

Only when the Lagonda looked exactly as it had done on the road, did she go down into the ferry's interior to check in with the time-keeper of the Great Road Race.

The vessel was well appointed, and she found the organisers and competitors all readying themselves for a lavish dinner in the restaurant. Ignoring the disbelief etched on the faces of the Carré-Dagneau family, she marched boldly up to Adélaïde and, remembering to reassume her American accent, said, "I've come to report the arrival on board of Devereux Lyminster's Lagonda. Its wheels touched the deck at nine forty-seven and twenty-three seconds."

Adélaïde Carré-Dagneau was so surprised that she did not question the information or ask how the car's arrival on board had been arranged. Lamely, she just entered the Lagonda's time on the check-sheets in her ledger. Neither she nor any other member of her family was too worried about this challenge to her precious Florian. Thanks to the delay before the ferry's departure, Blotto's team had still taken a good seventeen minutes longer than their nearest rivals.

Twinks spent the entire night on deck, awake in the driver's seat of the Lagonda. Her recent experiences had left her very wary of further attacks from French saboteurs. (Being Twinks, of course, she knew that the word "sabotage" came from the French *sabot*, meaning a worker's shoe. Being Twinks, she also knew that the widely held belief that the word derived from workers' habits of throwing shoes into machines to stop them working was erroneous etymology. She also knew, however, that the Carré-Dagneaux were quite capable of throwing a shoe into the Lagonda's engine.)

CHAPTER
NINE

La Jambe (The French Leg)

The ferry docked long before dawn, but few of the Great Road Race participants woke until seven. Their start was not until nine, and they wanted to be as rested and refreshed as possible for the day's challenges. Twinks had actually woken Blotto and Corky from their long slumbers at six thirty, feeling that nineteen and a half hours' sleep was probably enough.

While they were still assembling their scattered wits, she went to one of the ferry's luxurious bathrooms and changed from Ronald the Second Mechanic's white leathers into one of her own dresses in pale grey silk. And she removed her sequinned reticule from inside the young man's white leather satchel. She also produced a white cloche hat to keep her hair in place as the Lagonda blasted through the French countryside.

When she got back to the car, she found both men had woken fighting fit and extremely hungry. The Cherokee medicine man's remedy had done its stuff, removing all symptoms of their poisoning. Twinks suggested that they should both bathe and shave before hitting the substantial breakfast on offer in the restaurant.

By that time, there were sailors milling around on the deck and some of the mechanics from the other teams had arrived to tune their engines, so Twinks reckoned it was safe to leave the Lagonda unguarded. Unless all of the competitors were part of some huge conspiracy, further acts of sabotage would be observed and reported. She was hungry too, and tired after her sleepless vigil. She needed a huge infusion of breakfast to revive her flagging energy.

As the three of them walked down the companionway, Blotto said, "So you managed to get out of your 'educational' course in Scotland, did you, Twinks me old rust-remover?"

"*Nada problema*, Blotto me old lint-picker."

"I've forgotten . . . what was it you were bending the old brainbox around?"

"Water colours."

"Tickey-Tockey."

"But water hasn't got any colour," mumbled Corky Froggett resentfully. "That's the thing about water."

"Do you know, Twinkers, I actually have no recollection of driving the Lag on to the ferry?"

"That's what a good night's sleep can do for you, Blotters. Nothing like a touch of the old dreamless."

"You're bong on the nose there, Twinkers." Blotto stopped for a moment on the bottom step of the companionway. "Do you know, I would have sworn we had a second mechanic with us yesterday. Little boddo, about your height, American, dressed in white leather. Have you seen him around this morning?"

Twinks shook her head. "Maybe your sleep wasn't so dreamless after all."

"You mean he didn't exist? I dreamt the whole thing?"

"You've potted the black there, Blotters. That's exactly what must have happened."

"Ah. Strange, the tricks the old mind plays. I've clearly been suffering a touch of scrambling in the grey matter department."

"Give that pony a rosette!" said Twinks.

She caught Corky Froggett's eye and, unseen by Blotto, gave him a large wink. It was the chauffeur who had set up the appearance of Ronald the Second Mechanic.

As eight o'clock approached, the remaining six entrants in the Great Road Race were lined up across the Calais dockside. Without the facilities provided by Big Ben, Jean-Marie Carré-Dagneau was going to get the proceedings under way with a traditional starting pistol.

Blotto, fully restored to his customary super-fitness, was at the wheel of the Lagonda, and, before the start, he looked along the ranks of his rivals. It was a beautiful May day, and all of the cars had their tops down.

Though there were still more than ten minutes to go, Count Daspoontz was ready for the off, tensely bent over the steering wheel of his Krumpfenbach Big Eight, monocle gleaming in the sunlight and face fixed in the rictus of a snarl. His mechanics, with equally combative expressions, looked more like stormtroopers than ever.

In the Fettuccine roadster, Enrico Parmigiano-Reggiano and his acolytes exuded undiluted villainy. Blotto was uncomfortably reminded of time spent in a Chicago speakeasy with a gangster by the name of Spagsy Chiaparelli. He was determined to watch the Italian team as closely as snakes who'd slithered out of bed the wrong side that morning.

Blotto wasn't sure he trusted the American line-up too much either. The rugged openness of Brad Gimlet's face and the cleanliness of his two mechanics in their stars-and-stripes overalls looked almost too good to be true. Though by nature the most trusting of human beings, Blotto knew that things that looked too good to be true often were.

But of course, he could never believe anything bad about one of his old muffin-toasters from Eton. He looked across with confidence to where Trumbo McCorquodash lolled at the wheel of his Bentley, another magnum of champagne in his non-driving hand. Behind him, his two cousins, taking their cue from the older man, held smaller bottles of the good stuff. None of them was planning to let the thought of competition ruin a good day out. Blotto was warmed by the thought that there was still good in the world.

Then his eye stopped on Florian in the Florian, and his mood suddenly cooled. Though the events of the previous day were still a fog to him, there was evidence that morning that the original line-up of fifteen cars had been reduced by two-thirds. And he felt sure that, as organisers of the Great Road Race, the Carré-Dagneau family must have had something to do with that culling. Their determination to win was stronger than any considerations of honour or morality. They were, after all, French.

Blotto was still musing darkly — well, not that darkly; things never got really dark for Blotto — when the voice of his sister drew him back to reality. "Blotto me old tin of boot polish — and Corky — I've got something for both of you."

"Oh?" said her brother blankly. The chauffeur said nothing, but Twinks knew she had his full attention.

She reached into her sequinned reticule and produced two small leather wallets, one of which she handed to each of the men. "A few necessaries in case we get separated."

"What kind of 'necessaries'?" asked Blotto suspiciously.

"Some French francs, a torch, set of spanners, that kind of clangdumble. Never know when you'll need them."

"Tickey-Tockey," said her brother.

"Thank you very much, milady," said Corky, slipping the wallet into the back pocket of his uniform trousers.

Twinks took her stopwatch out of her sequinned reticule, checked its reading and said to Blotto, "You realise we've got quite a lot to make up today?"

"'Make-up'? I don't wear make-up."

"No, I know that, Blotters."

"Boddoes who wear make-up are way the wrong side of the running rail."

"I'm talking about time we have to make up, not makeup to put on your face."

"Ah. On the same page, Twinkers."

86

"Because of our late arrival on the ferry last night, we're shy of the Carré-Dagneau Florian by sixteen minutes and eleven seconds."

"Well, I'll be jugged like a hare! How did we manage to cobble the clock by that much?"

Twinks was still undecided about how much she wanted to divulge about the night before. She wasn't being deliberately secretive. It was just that explaining the whole sequence of events — and probably having to explain a lot of it twice for Blotto to catch up — would take an inordinately long time. And she did feel very tired.

Fortunately, the decision to tell or not to tell at that moment was taken from her, as the report of Jean-Marie Carré-Dagneau's starting pistol echoed across the dockside, and her brother uncaged the power of the Lagonda.

Even Blotto had to admit that the French countryside didn't look bad. Not, obviously, anything like as good as the rural delights of Tawcestershire, but none too dusty, all the same, in the April sunshine. Knowing that the English drove on the left side of the road and the French drove on the wrong side, Blotto compromised by driving straight down the middle. The undoubted pleasure of sending walkers and horse-drawn vehicles scattering and scuttling into the hedgerows proved to be as rewarding as it was back in the old country. French peasants were just as slow at getting out of the way as their English counterparts. Blotto always found driving along roads chasing pedestrians had the same appeal as hunting foxes.

There was a kind of primitive charm to the villages the Lagonda roared through. Ancient churches, quaint markets and houses at various stages of dilapidation. He was surprised to see how many of the buildings had large advertisements painted on their walls. These were mostly for noxious alcoholic drinks, but there were also some for car manufacturers. A lot, he noticed, promoted the wares of Les Automobiles Carré-Dagneau. How unbelievably vulgar, he thought, drawing attention to oneself in that way. Any sort of publicity is the last refuge of a scoundrel.

But, as he continued to put more miles between his Lagonda and the chasing pack, Blotto felt very benign. His emotional barometer had returned to its customary setting of "Sunny". And he knew that, if Twinks hadn't been catching up on the previous night's sleep, she would be as cheerful as he was, expressing herself with frequent cries of "Jollissimo!", "Grandissimo!" and "Larksissimo!"

Corky Froggett, though, he could see in his rear-view mirror, was not sharing the ecstatic mood. Blotto hadn't a clue why this should be. Twinks, blessed with more instinctive sensitivity, would have suspected that being in France brought back to the chauffeur painful memories of his encounters with the lovely Yvette, and the subsequent rekindling of romance when he met her as Madame Clothilde of Mayfair. But since she was asleep, she said nothing.

Her brother, though, was rarely so restrained. "What's put lumps in your custard, Corky?" he demanded. "You're looking a bit crabwhacked. Is it being back among the garlic-guzzlers that's brought you out in crimps?"

"I must confess, milord," came the reply, "that making a return visit to France has upset my customary equilibrium."

"Memories of one of the gentler gender, is it?" suggested Blotto sympathetically.

"No, milord. My discomfort arises from the fact that, last time I was in this country, I was equipped with a Vickers machine-gun and licensed to do the most important thing that I was put on this earth to do — in other words, to shoot people!"

"Ah, yes. I can see that might be a bit of a stye in the eye for you, Corky."

Realising that, in his passion, he might have gone too far, the chauffeur backtracked a little. "When I said it was the most important thing that I was put on this earth to do, I did of course mean it was the *second* most important thing I was put on this earth to do. The *first* was to serve you, milord, in any capacity which might be required — even to the point of sacrificing my life for you. Which I would do readily, should a suitable opportunity arise."

"Good ticket," murmured Blotto.

Remembering that there were three people in the Lagonda, Corky added, "And I would, needless to say, do the same for you, milady."

Just at that moment, Twinks awoke. "You've always been a Grade A foundation stone, Corky," she mumbled sleepily.

"Thank you, milady."

In seconds she was fully awake. She pulled the white cloche hat down over her ears, and her eyes shone with even more than their usual sparkle as she surveyed the flat terrain of Northern France. She watched with glee as a peasant's wagon, loaded with barrels, was forced into a roadside ditch, sending its cargo scattering. "Oh, isn't this splendissimo, Blotters!" she cried. "Now we really are rolling on camomile lawns! And I'm sure we're whittling away at that sixteen minutes and eleven seconds."

It goes without saying that Twinks had done a great deal of homework on finding the shortest route between Calais and the Carré-Dagneaux's Château d'Igeaux. The quality of her planning was superior to that of the other competitors, which meant that her chosen route was some twenty minutes shorter than theirs. That advantage, coupled with the Lagonda's power and Blotto's driving skills, meant they felt confident of cutting down the time deficit caused by dirty doings at Dover.

The English team were unsurprised to arrive at the Château d'Igeaux ahead of all the opposition. Having flown down in the Giselle, Madame Carré-Dagneau had of course got there before them, but she was not at the check-in table when they crossed the moat to the Château's imposing main gates. Twinks, who of course

90

had been keeping their time with the stopwatch from her sequinned reticule, summoned the gate-keeper and, in fluent French, insisted that he made the appropriate entry in the ledger on the table. Far too cowed by her beauty to disagree, he was then despatched by a patrician command from Twinks to fetch his mistress.

Adélaïde Carré-Dagneau was clearly annoyed to have been caught out. She had not expected any of the cars to arrive so soon. She was also extremely annoyed by the identity of the first arrival. She did little to hide her disappointment that the first car hadn't been her precious son's Florian. But she had no alternative but to confirm the Lagonda's time, as entered accurately by the gate-keeper.

To her continuing annoyance, the English team hung around near her check-in point, waiting to see who would come in second. Once they'd got the next car's time, they would be able to work out how much they still had to make up.

However much she resented their presence, though, Madame Carré-Dagneau was sufficiently aware of her duties as a hostess to organise staff champagne for her unwanted guests. Because of his lowly status, Corky Froggett was not offered a glass. He wouldn't have accepted it anyway. After the dodgy Coquilles-St-Jacques at the Savoy, he was determined to be on his guard against any future attempts at sabotage. He was, he kept reminding himself, among the perfidious French, who were capable of any kind of double-dealing. (He also had to keep reminding himself that England and France had been on the same side during the recent little dust-up with the Hun. It was something he had a habit of forgetting. Though he reckoned, given France's previous form in such matters, it was an easy mistake to make.)

Blotto and Twinks, meanwhile, sat on the running board of the Lagonda, sunning themselves as they sipped the Carré-Dagneaux's excellent champagne. They drank in the beauty of the château. It was built around a square courtyard, with a central formal garden and fountain, but enough room on the gravel around it to park all the cars from the Great Road Race. (It would actually have provided sufficient space for all of the original entrants, had Gallic skulduggery at Dover not so diminished their numbers.)

The Château d'Igeaux had been built beside a small river, whose flow had been diverted to form its moat. At each of its four corners were towers with pointed caps on top. Blotto was of the view that such architectural flourishes were mere indulgence. The word "château", he'd understood from the beaks at Eton, was supposed to mean "castle", and for him a castle should have towers with flat tops and crenellations. A bit like Tawcester Towers. Very like Tawcester Towers. In fact, in every way Tawcester Towers was the archetype of what the word "castle" meant. It was typical of the mimsy-pimsy French to stick upturned ice-cream cones on top of their towers and have the nerve to call the result a "château".

Twinks, who had a little more aesthetic discrimination than her brother, thought the Château d'Igeaux was very beautiful.

At the end of the French leg of the Great Road Race, there was a change in the order from the previous day. The first car to reach Dover had been the Fettuccine roadster. But it was beaten to second place at the Château d'Igeaux by the Americans' Cadebaker, which came in eleven minutes and nineteen seconds after the arrival of the Lagonda.

The Italian team were two minutes and thirty-two seconds behind them. Twinks didn't need to retrieve the abacus from her sequinned reticule to work out that the Lagonda was now only three minutes and twenty seconds behind the previous day's leaders. And, because of the difference in time on the craning of the two vehicles at Dover, the Italians still had an overall lead. But that didn't worry the English team. Winning the Great Road Race, they felt confident, was going to be as easy as swatting a mozzy.

The Brits weren't interested in the timings of the other competitors and were unsurprised that there was no sign of Trumbo McCorquodash's Bentley. Blotto could guess the reason. It would have been completely out of character for Trumbo to travel through France without stopping for a lavish champagne-fuelled *menu gastronomique* at some recommended restaurant. And he was probably still there.

The competitors went off to find the lavish accommodation provided for them in the Château d'Igeaux and dress for dinner. Corky Froggett was not the only mechanic to stay with his vehicle. Compared to the level of distrust felt for the Carré-Dagneaux, Judas was one of the good guys.

CHAPTER
TEN

Dinner at the Château

"It is to me a matter of profound regret," announced Jean-Marie Carré-Dagneau, "that I hear some people suffered ill-effects from the dinner the night before the start of the Great Road Race."

Some boddoes do like the sound of their own voices, thought Blotto. The breakfast in Calais was a long time ago, he was hungry after his day's driving and wanted to get on with dinner. He wasn't worried about the prospect of further gut-gripes. His ever-resourceful sister had in her sequinned reticule a poison-detecting device of her own design which, in tests, had been proved to be 99.99999999 per cent accurate.

"I also regret," the automobile manufacturer went on, "that the standards of hygiene in the Savoy kitchens should have proved so unreliable as to have led to this outbreak of food poisoning."

Now rein in the roans there a moment, thought Blotto. You can't say that kind of thing about the Sawers — particularly when the menu that night was knocked up by your own chef. He was about to vocalise his objection, when he spotted a deterrent shake of the head from Twinks. Reluctantly, he reconciled himself with not rising to the insult. His sister always knew best in such circumstances.

It soon became clear they were not the only ones suspicious of the Carré-Dagneau catering, as the head of the family continued, "Anyway, you need have no worries tonight about the quality of the food from the Château d'Igeaux kitchens. Of course, you would have no worries under any circumstances, but our good friends the American team . . ." He nodded towards them and received a blinding flash of teeth from Brad Gimlet ". . . have insisted on having all of the dishes on this evening's menu *tasted* by one of their junior mechanics. This is obviously an unnecessary precaution . . ." He spoke through gritted teeth. ". . . but I am willing to accept any over-cautious and frankly offensive restrictions to maintain the harmony between our two great nations."

More teeth gleamed from the American table.

"Even if that nation did prove rather dilatory in coming to our aid during the last war." The American teeth stopped gleaming.

"And now, let us all enjoy our dinner, in a fine spirit of *camaraderie* . . ." (Idly, Blotto wondered what the French for *camaraderie* was.) ". . . and look forward to the competition continuing in the morning."

As Jean-Marie Carré-Dagneau sat down, waiters appeared instantly with bowls of *consommé*. (Idly, Blotto wondered what the French for *consommé* was.) Once the soup had been tasted by the American mechanic — and he'd been given a minute to see if he dropped dead, which he didn't — the dinner guests settled down to eating.

Unlike at the Savoy, where the teams had been seated in individual groups, that evening's dinner was served at one long table in the château's banqueting hall. The *placement* (idly, Blotto wondered what the French for *placement* was) had seated him next to the pouting sulkiness of Giselle Carré-Dagneau. She wore a black dress that seemed to be all fringes and beads, with an improbably low neckline. For a moment Blotto considered offering her his jacket to cover it up but decided against the idea. He didn't want to draw attention to her sartorial impropriety.

He looked across the table to see that Twinks hadn't done much better in terms of *placement*. She had been seated next to the person who gave moustaches a bad name, Florian Carré-Dagneau. Blotto caught his sister's eye. The looks exchanged suggested neither of them anticipated having any fun that evening.

Blotto, with the French girl on one side and an Italian mechanic on the other, did not expect much in the way of conversation. He knew no Italian and, though the beaks at Eton had put much effort into cramming French into his brain, after every lesson he found it had all trickled out by the time he had left the classroom.

He was therefore considerably surprised, as he took his first spoonful of *consommé*, to hear a female voice on his right speak to him in English. "So, should I call you 'Devereux Lyminster' or 'Monsieur Lyminster' or 'Lord Lyminster'?" Giselle had a heavy accent, but her

English was very correct. Evidently, a lot of the Carré-Dagneau millions had been spent on sending her to the right schools (though, from the loftiness of an Eton education, Blotto rather wondered whether there were any "right" schools in France).

"Most boddoes just call me 'Blotto'," he confessed.

"'Blotto'? This is charming, no?"

"Well, it's, you know, the label that's been hung round my neck since I was in nursery-naps." He'd never really thought whether it was "charming" or not. Now he did think about it, he thought it probably wasn't.

"But, Blotto, *I* think it is charming, your name."

"Tickey-Tockey. And Giselle . . . that's a . . . well . . . That's your name."

"Yes."

Blotto was rather stumped for something else to say. "Erm . . ." He floundered, desperately. "'Giselle' sounds a little like 'gazelle'."

"A little, yes."

"A gazelle's a kind of antelope." Blotto's range of knowledge was not broad, but he was quite good on the names of animals that could be shot.

"I know that, Blotto."

"Ah." He wasn't finding this easy. "So, what's the French for 'gazelle'?"

"*Gazelle.*"

"Ah. Good ticket. Nearly the same word."

"Nearly, yes."

Another silence. Blotto tried desperately to think of something else to say. "Of course, if all words were the same in English and French, then we wouldn't have to learn foreign languages, would we?"

"No."

"Save an awful lot of trouble, wouldn't it?"

"Yes."

Blotto looked Giselle in the eyes for the first time. "Didn't you find it difficult, when you were in nursery-naps, growing up speaking a foreign language? Presumably your parents insisted you did. It seems a particularly cruel thing to do to a child."

"I did not think of it as a foreign language."

"Didn't you? What, nobody told you?" Blotto was appalled. "I mean, I don't want to cast nasturtiums on your aged Ps, but that seems a bit murdy of them."

"I did not think so."

"No?" An even more appalling thought struck Blotto. "I say, didn't your parents even tell you that you were foreign?"

But, perhaps because she did not wish to express criticism of her parents, Giselle did not answer this question. Instead, looking him straight in the eyes, she said, "You know, I have been watching you, Blotto, since we first met."

"Great Wilberforce, have you? But that's not very long, is it? You only clapped your peepers on me two nights ago."

"But do you not believe that there are some people, who, when you see them for the first time, you feel as if you have known them for ever?"

Blotto had always prided himself on giving a straight answer to a straight question. "No," he replied. "I always find, when I'm seeing someone for the first time, I'm seeing them for the first time."

"Oh." Giselle sounded a little downcast. "So, when you first saw me, did you not feel a little *frisson*?"

"No," he replied with his customary honesty. Idly, Blotto wondered what the French was for *frisson*.

"When I first saw you, Blotto, at the Savoy, I felt something very strange."

"Ah," he responded. "Was it the Coquilles-St-Jacques?" This was an interesting idea. If she had also suffered food poisoning, then he'd have completely to rethink his Carré-Dagneau family conspiracy theory.

"It was not the Coquilles-St-Jacques," said Giselle. "It was something I felt *here*." She pressed a hand against her generous bosom.

"Really? I have to say it got me a lot lower down."

"But why are we talking of Coquilles-St-Jacques? I speak of something much more powerful than that."

"Oh, well, I thought the old Coquilles-St-Jacques were pretty powerful. I mean, I spent the whole spoffing night rushing —"

"No," Giselle interrupted him, and said with some insistence, "I do not refer to the Coquilles-St-Jacques, I refer to something that we in France call a *coup de foudre*. Do you know what this means, Blotto?"

Rather than admit that he didn't, he hazarded, "Something to do with food, is it?" He beamed as he had a rather clever thought. "Indigestion?"

"No." Her eyelashes were fluttering a lot. He didn't like to mention the fact because he thought it might be some kind of unfortunate tic. Doesn't do to mock the afflicted. "Do you know what love is, Blotto?"

"Oh yes," he replied, glad that the questions were getting easier.

"And what is it?"

"It's the score when you're making a gumbo of things on the tennis court."

She laughed a tinkling laugh, as if what he'd just said was deliberately funny.

"No, it is," he insisted.

"Perhaps it will be more meaningful for you if I mention the word *amour*. Do you know what *amour* is, Blotto?"

"You bet your bootstraps I do!"

"So, what is it?" she asked coquettishly.

A distant memory of something said by an English beak at Eton bubbled to the blank surface of his mind. "It's a boddo who comes from North Africa. As in *Othello, Amour of Venice*, what? A play written by Milton or one of that lot."

"I am not familiar with English literature," said Giselle.

"Join the club," said Blotto.

"But that is not what *l'amour* is."

"Really?" Another distant recollection from the Etonian schoolroom came to him. "By Cheddar, is it a cupboard?"

"No, Blotto, it is not. But, for a Frenchwoman," Giselle Carré-Dagneau breathed, "*l'amour* is everything."

"Tickey-Tockey."

"For *l'amour*, I will give up all other demands on my time."

"Good ticket. I'm a bit like that with cricket."

"Do you know, Blotto . . ." He couldn't quite understand why she felt it necessary to lean so close to him. Maybe she thought he was deaf. "I have something of a reputation as a *femme fatale*."

"Do you, by Denzil?" He had heard the expression. Idly, Blotto wondered what was the French for *femme fatale*.

"Would you like to find out why I have this reputation?"

More misty recollections from the classroom told him that in Latin there were two kinds of questions — those expecting the answer "Yes" and those expecting the answer "No". He recognised Giselle's as one of the former and was far too well brought up to do other than provide the required answer.

"*C'est formidable!*" she murmured. "Knock on the door of my *boudoir* at midnight."

He knew what a "*boudoir*" was. Twinks had got one. Idly, Blotto wondered what the French for *boudoir* was.

At the other side of the table, Florian Carré-Dagneau appeared not to have much in the way of English. This suited Twinks well. Though her French was of course perfect, she had no particular desire to talk to someone who looked as though a hairy caterpillar was crawling across his upper lip.

101

But the *placement* had set on her other side one of Count Daspoontz's mechanics, who was so Teutonically monosyllabic that, in spite of her of course perfect German, conversation with him was an uphill struggle. So, out of sheer boredom and the knowledge that she could not politely leave the table until at least the dessert course, she found herself talking to Florian; though, actually, *listening* to Florian might be a more accurate description.

Because, despite the many shortcomings he had in the looks and charm department, the one thing the young driver did not seem to lack was self-assurance. Self-assurance bordering on arrogance. No, self-assurance spilling way over the brim of arrogance.

Twinks knew, from long experience, that what men mostly wanted to talk about was themselves. On first meeting her, some of them were sufficiently distracted from their specialist subject by her beauty to spend a little time in making crass compliments. But they all pretty quickly tired of talking about her and got back to talking about themselves. And trying to convince her how their prowess in various fields of masculine endeavour qualified them uniquely as partners for her. This oft-repeated routine was, Twinks recognised wearily, a hazard of her utter gorgeousness.

Florian Carré-Dagneau, however, was different. He didn't bother with the customary detour about her, he just went straight to talking about Florian Carré-Dagneau. Whether he knew any English or not, he made no concessions to the nationality of his audience.

102

He talked as if the privilege of the conversation was all hers.

"I will of course," he said (in French), "be a very famous racing driver. This Great Road Race will just be the first of many triumphs —"

"Erm," Twinks interrupted, "just a momentette . . . You haven't won the Great Road Race yet, have you?"

"This is a detail," said Florian airily. "There is no way I cannot win."

You may think that, Twinks thought, but did not vocalise. And you may think that by poisoning the other competitors and preventing them from getting on ferries, your dream will be realised. But what you haven't reckoned on is that you are up against Blotto and Twinks, and that means you've as much hope as a butter pat in a blast furnace.

"I am not only a great driver," he continued, "I am also a great lover."

"Are you?" said Twinks.

"Yes. All the women in France wish to have me as their lover."

"Do they?" said Twinks. "Well, there is no accounting for tastes."

"My mother tells me I should marry, but I do not think I am ready for this yet."

"You're bong on the nose there, Florian," said Twinks, of the view that he probably wasn't yet ready to leave the nursery.

"Why, Twinks, should I devote my life to focusing on one bloom, however beautiful, when there are so many flowers in the garden?"

"Yes, a lot of insects have that attitude," said Twinks.

But Florian Carré-Dagneau was too firmly encased in his carapace of self-admiration to be aware of any insults. He now focused his eyes on Twinks's face and said in a tone as creamy as a *béchamel* sauce, "You are a very beautiful woman."

With most of the many British amorous swains who addressed her in these words, her response would be, "Don't talk such toffee!" But, faced with the French arrogance of Florian Carré-Dagneau, she just said, "Yes. I know."

"You would perhaps wish to be my lover?"

"I'd rather have my peepers removed and served up to me in minestrone soup," she replied, reasonably enough.

Clearly, his ears had some kind of filtration system which prevented them from hearing anything to his disadvantage, because he went on, "I think perhaps I could arrange something . . ."

"Don't strain your sinews on my account."

"I would say 'come up to my bedroom', but this is perhaps not a good idea."

"Oh, really? Why not?" asked Twinks, her voice heavy with unnoticed sarcasm.

"If other women see I have chosen you to come up to my bedroom, they will become very jealous, I think."

"Do you?"

"No. It will be better if we meet at my father's study."

"Oh?"

"Yes, it is on this floor, at the back of the Château. Behind the library. Normally, he keeps it firmly locked, but I have a key and will see to it that the door opens when you arrive." He snuffled that peculiarly French laugh which is mostly a snort. "And, do not worry, next to the study my father has a bedroom . . . a place where he can go, when the stresses of business become too great, to be pleasured by one of his mistresses. That is how Frenchmen behave, always have. The Frenchman is designed to have many mistresses. And my father is French, of course, like me. I am very French."

"Well, there's a surprise," said Twinks.

"So, would you like to go to my father's study?"

"Yes, I spoffing well would." The opportunity to do a little snooping into the business dealings of the Carré-Dagneaux was too good to miss.

"And would you like me to join you there?"

"Don't mind if you don't."

But again, his ear-filter of self-esteem stopped him from hearing that.

"At midnight," Florian Carré-Dagneau breathed sexily.

At least he thought he sounded sexy. To Twinks, he sounded like an asthmatic blowing up a balloon.

CHAPTER
ELEVEN

Night Manoeuvres at
the Château

There was no heating in the Lagonda, but the April night was warm, and Corky Froggett had survived worse. He actually found it strange being in France without the feeling of trench mud seeping through the fabric of his puttees.

And he wasn't daunted by the prospect of spending the night awake in the car. Any suffering he underwent in the cause of the Young Master was fine by him. Obviously, he'd rather be laying down his life, but until that magic moment came, he'd have to make do, by way of suffering, with cramp in his calves and a bit of back pain. Blotto would be doing all the driving to Monaco the next day, so Corky could catch up on his sleep then.

He looked at the other cars glinting in the thin moonlight. Still just four competitors — the Krumpfenbach, the Cadebaker, the Fettuccine roadster and, of course, the Florian. Corky smiled the smile of a man who knew that the Lagonda could easily thrash the lot of them.

There was one other vehicle parked in the Château courtyard. The Adélaïde, the largest and most luxurious model produced by Les Automobiles Carré-Dagneau, It was in this that its namesake and her husband — and probably their daughter — would, after the competing cars had departed, be driven to the nearest airstrip, to be flown in the Carré-Dagneau Giselle to Monaco.

A knock on the Lagonda's window brought the chauffeur out of his reverie. Instantly, his service pistol was in his hand as he lowered the glass and looked out.

Outlined in the moonlight, he saw the generous figure of a woman, comfortably dressed in a maid's uniform. He put away his pistol and took out the electric torch from the wallet Twinks had given him in Calais. Its beam focused on the maid's plump and smiling face. It also illuminated a tray, on which she carried a bottle of wine and a glass. "Good evening, monsieur," she said.

Her appearance and her words had a profound effect on Corky. When he had first met the fabled Yvette in a café near Arras, she had been similarly dressed. There was something about maids' uniforms that never failed to excite him. And Yvette's first words to him had also been: "Good evening, monsieur."

He remembered enough French to say, "Good evening, mademoiselle."

"I saw you out here alone in the car." Her accent was heavy, but her English was good. Just as Yvette's had been. "And I thought, ah, the poor man. I must take some drink to him. And then some food. You have not had the dinner, no?"

Corky admitted that he hadn't.

"Then, here, take this." She handed the tray across. The cork had been extracted from the bottle and stuffed back in. "You can open this, I think, yes?"

"I think, yes," said the chauffeur enthusiastically.

"Then pour yourself a glass. I will go back to the kitchens and fetch your dinner."

"Thank you very much," said Corky.

"And then, perhaps . . ." The woman winked. "I can join you in the car . . . for a glass of wine . . . or something . . . This will be all right, yes?"

"This will be very much all right, yes."

"*A bientôt*," The woman blew him a kiss. "Soon, I will bring you your dinner . . . and not just your dinner . . ."

Corky Froggett grinned. Every individual hair of his moustache bristled with anticipation. He swallowed down his first glass of wine in a single gulp and poured another one. Maybe France wasn't going to be so bad, after all.

The woman did not return with his dinner. But he wouldn't have been able to eat it anyway. He was only halfway through his second glass when the sedative in the wine took effect.

Twinks knew that her assignation with Florian was for midnight, but she made her way to Jean-Marie Carré-Dagneau's study at eleven fifteen, hoping that the young man had already unlocked the door. If he had, she could have done all the snooping she required and be safely back in her own bed before he arrived.

Her luck was in. The heavy door opened easily as she turned the handle. (In fact, even if the door had been locked, it would have offered no real problem for Twinks. In her sequinned reticule she had a set of picklocks which could enable her to enter the most diligently protected of strongholds.)

But she still reached into the reticule. Not knowing where the windows were in Jean-Marie Carré-Dagneau's study, she was not going to risk putting the lights on. Needless to say, she possessed a small but powerful electric torch for just such eventualities.

Jean-Marie Carré-Dagneau was clearly a man of tidy habits. There was not a single sheet of paper visible on any of the study's surfaces. The walls were lined with dark wood fitted cupboards, all no doubt full of interesting documents, but Twinks decided to concentrate first on the desk. This, Twinks recognised (because she knew all about furniture, as well as everything else) was a fine rosewood secretaire from the Louis XV period, decorated in marquetry of brass, tortoiseshell and bronze. There was a central drawer above the well, and two on each side.

(She had noticed that the Château d'Igeaux was full of antiques, but she did not think they were Carré-Dagneau heirlooms. They had been bought, lock, stock and barrel, with the Château itself. As a Lyminster with authentic family history, she was quick to identify those who had none; those who suffered the indignity of having bought rather than inherited their furniture. The father from whom Jean-Marie Carré-Dagneau had inherited the company had been nothing more than a bicycle mechanic who got lucky. The Carré-Dagneaux had no pre-Revolutionary title, though probably in time Jean-Marie would buy himself one. No, the family were irredeemably *nouveau riche*. Sadly, Blotto wasn't present to wonder idly what the French was for *nouveau riche*.)

For the drawers of the secretaire, Twinks did need to extract the picklocks from her sequinned reticule. She opened the central one first. She had anticipated going through piles of account ledgers, sales figures and vehicle blueprints before she found anything of interest, and indeed she wasn't quite sure what would be "of interest". She just had a gut feeling that there was something criminal in the set-up of Les Automobiles Carré-Dagneau, However, as it turned out, she hit pay-dirt straight away.

The first documents she found were mock-ups of advertisements for the new Carré-Dagneau Florian. Against the blue of the Mediterranean, the car was shown speeding along the roads of the Corniche. A young man, fortunately looking nothing like Florian Carré-Dagneau, was driving nonchalantly, with an arm round the slender shoulders of a stunning blonde in a cloche hat.

But it was not the image that interested Twinks, it was the text. She didn't care about the technical details, the number of litres the engine boasted or its revolutionary suspension system. Nor did the list of dealers where she could purchase a Florian concern her. It was the headline:

THE NEW CARRÉ-DAGNEAU FLORIAN
WINNER OF THE GREAT ROAD RACE!

Jean-Marie and his crew were very definitely counting their chickens before they were hatched. Unless, of course, they knew for a fact that Florian Carré-Dagneau in the Florian was certain to triumph. Given the way they had tried to sabotage the opposition, such an outcome was not beyond the realms of possibility.

Twinks looked further through the documentation. There were not just mock-ups of the posters, but also designs to be painted, in that peculiarly French form of advertising, on the sides of houses. There were ads to be printed in newspapers and magazines, along with flyers to be pasted on to the exterior of every urinal in France. And all of them made the same claim — that the Florian had won the Great Road Race.

Twinks was shocked by the sheer effrontery of it. How dare the Carré-Dagneaux count their blue tits before they were born? She was more than ever determined that justice should triumph, and that the Lagonda would be the first car to cross that finish line in Rome.

But under all the advertising copy, she found something to make her blood boil even more furiously. It was a carbon copy of part of a letter. Only the second page, so she could not tell to whom it was addressed. But underneath the space at the bottom for the signature was printed: "M. Jean-Marie Carré-Dagneau, Directeur Général, Les Automobiles Carré-Dagneau".

The contents were of course in French, but that posed no problem for Twinks; it was one of the many languages she spoke like a native. The page started halfway through a sentence and read:

. . . ensure that there are by then no challengers to the Florian.

I am not concerned what methods you use to achieve this outcome, so long as none of the necessary criminal acts can be directly attributed to anyone in the Carré-Dagneau family or any employees of Les Automobiles Carré-Dagneau.

As you pointed out, the victory will not only give an enormous boost to sales of our new model, it will also ensure that we do not have to pay out the ten thousand pounds in gold sovereigns which have been offered to the victor. A win-win situation for us, which will mean that my company gains an enormous publicity bonus for a relatively modest outlay.

A win-win situation for you too, of course. You will be paid the agreed fee as soon as the Florian crosses the finish line by the Colosseum. I still feel the price you negotiated was a staggeringly high one, but if you fulfil yours, I will be happy to fulfil my side of the bargain.

I make no strictures on the methods you use by which to achieve our mutually desired ends. I would ask you to avoid murder, only because it could raise the prospect of too close an investigation of my business affairs. But if the odd killing is necessary — and I know you can call on many members of your organisation skilled in such evil arts — so long as it is done discreetly, I will raise no objections. The commercial climate in which I operate is a vicious one, in which we cannot be impeded by old-fashioned considerations of morality.

This is the last time I will communicate directly with you. Should our paths cross in the course of the Great Road Race, I will betray no signs of ever having met you before, and I rely on you to do the same. Your fee will be paid through our appointed intermediary in Rome, as discussed at our last meeting.

I won't say it's a pleasure to do business with you or an institution like yours, but it is a course of whose necessity I'm sure we are both aware.

Yours sincerely . . .

The slugbucket! thought Twinks. If Jean-Marie Carré-Dagneau thinks he can get away with that, then he's very definitely shinnying up the wrong drainpipe! If he thinks he's going to win the Great Road Race by employing a bunch of blunderthugs who don't mind coffinating the odd boddo, then he's certainly plumping for the wrong plum. And what, for the love of strawberries, does "an institution like yours" mean? It must be some kind of criminal org —

She was stopped in mid-thought by the sound of the study door opening. She looked up to see who had arrived.

As Blotto mounted the stairs towards Giselle Carré-Dagneau's *boudoir*, he conjectured about what might lie ahead. She had promised to show him why she had a reputation as a *femme fatale*. Apart from idly wondering what was the French for *femme fatale*, he also idly wondered what *femme fatale* meant. It wasn't a topic that had been covered in the Eton French syllabus. But he did know that "*femme*" meant some kind of fish.

No, was he right about that, though? He knew he had, from time to time, in overpriced London restaurants, been served up with some frenchified dish called "*sole bonne femme*", but he wasn't sure which bit of that name was the fish. Assuming the French word bore some relation to the English — an assumption that could certainly not always be made — perhaps the fish bit was the "*sole*" . . .? He knew that "*bonne*" meant "good". So, what did the "*femme*" bit mean?

Woman! Suddenly, it came back to him. So . . . something about a woman . . .? "*Fatale* . . . ?" What could that mean? Working on the same principle as he had with the "*sole*", "*fatale*" might have something to do with "*fatal*" . . .?

A woman fatal? A fatal woman? By Wilberforce, did this mean that Giselle Carré-Dagneau was a trained assassin? Toad-in-the-hole! Blotto wished he had thought to bring his cricket bat with him.

Further speculation was halted by his arrival at the *boudoir*. As he raised his knuckles but before he had

114

time to knock, the door was opened and the slender hand of Giselle Carré-Dagneau drew him inside.

Blotto's experience of *boudoirs* was limited. Twinks's was the only one with which he had any real familiarity, and he was amazed by the difference between that and the room he had just entered. Twinks's retreat at Tawcester Towers seemed to him quite sufficiently fluffy and girlish, but it could have been a nun's cell compared to the space where Giselle Carré-Dagneau conducted her most intimate activities. Every wall was covered with panels of painting or tapestry. No doorway was uncrowned by a statue of nymphs and shepherds. Anything that could be gilded was gilded, and every wooden surface was decorated with elaborate marquetry.

Blotto's reaction to the space was rather like his reaction to French food. It was all too fussy, with far too many ingredients. The *boudoir* gave him visual indigestion.

Giselle Carré-Dagneau seemed unaware of his discomfiture. After letting him in, she had crossed the room to drape herself over a *chaise longue*, which was as over-decorated as everything else in the room. She had changed out of her black dinner dress and was now sporting a cream silk *negligée*. (Idly, Blotto wondered what the French was for *negligée*.) The neckline on this garment threatened to expose her navel.

Remembering his manners, Blotto performed the act of gallantry which the public nature of the banqueting hall had prevented him from performing. He whipped off his dinner jacket and proffered it towards Giselle.

115

"I am sorry . . . what is this?"

"I thought you must've had a bit of an egg-scramble in the wardrobe department. Might like to cover it up . . .?"

"'Cover it up'? Why should I wish to cover it up?"

"I don't know. Just a thoughtette."

"Do you not like what you see, Blotto?" Giselle asked in a sultry tone.

He once again took stock of the room. "A bit too much of a good thing, perhaps . . .?" he suggested.

Giselle, who had not seen where he had been looking, chuckled fruitily. "There are some 'good things', Blotto, of which it is impossible to have too much."

"Tickey-Tockey," he said emolliently. He had no wish to get into an argument with the poor little thimble.

"Blotto," she susurrated, patting the small area of *chaise longue* that she was not draped over, "why don't you come and join me more closely . . . since you already have your jacket off . . . ready for action . . .?"

"Oh, pardon my pickle," said Blotto, putting his jacket back on.

"Blotto, I do not think we are . . . how do you say it? Seeing eye to eye?"

"No, well, that's because I'm standing up and you're sitting down."

"I think it is very easy for you to solve this problem." She once again patted the small triangle of vacant *chaise longue*.

116

Blotto crossed the room to scrutinise the fabric she was indicating. "What is the problem?" he asked. "Moths?"

" 'Moths'? Why should there be 'moths' on my *chaise longue*?"

"The little pinkers do like eating cloth, you know. No snackette a moth likes better than a spoffing cloth sandwich."

"But surely, 'moths' is not an animal?"

"Sorry? I'm afraid my touch paper hasn't ignited yet."

" 'Moths'," she explained, "is something which grows on things. As in your English saying: 'A rolling stone gathers no moths'."

Blotto didn't correct her mistake. He just thought again how perverse it was for the French not to bring up their children speaking English. It would have simplified things so much.

Giselle Carré-Dagneau was signally failing in her attempts to get him on to the *chaise longue* with her, so she tried another approach. She stood up and moved very close. "Blotto," she murmured, "would you like to see my . . . inner sanctum?"

Blotto was perplexed. He would not claim to be an expert on female anatomy, and he could not have put a finger on where the "inner sanctum" was. But he reckoned he was already seeing quite enough of Giselle's body in her plunging *décolletage*. (Idly, Blotto wondered what the French for *décolletage* was.) He thought the prospect of her revealing her "inner sanctum" could only be embarrassing.

"Well, er," he said, "time for me to be pongling bedwards."

"I couldn't agree more," purred Giselle.

"Jump into the jim-jams," he said, backing towards the door, "and shut the peepers for a bit of the old beauty stuff."

"No," said Giselle, reaching out a hand and grasping his with surprising strength. "You must see my inner sanctum."

"I think that might be a bit beyond the barbed wire for most boddoes," Blotto objected.

But Giselle was not to be gainsaid. Still keeping a firm hold of his hand with one of her own, she used the other to turn a decorative angel which was affixed to the wall. Instantly, a panel slid back to reveal the metal grid of a lift door.

"This used to be a small staircase," she explained, "by which the lovers of the *châtelaine* would leave when she had finished with them. My father had it replaced by this elevator."

She clanked the gate open and pushed Blotto forcibly into the lift.

"Where are you taking me?" he asked uneasily.

"I told you," said Giselle, as she clanked the gate shut. "To see my inner sanctum."

"Toad-in-the-hole!" said Blotto.

CHAPTER
TWELVE

Chicanery at the Château

The person who had joined Twinks in Jean-Marie Carré-Dagneau's study was, unsurprisingly, his son.

"Good evening, Florian," she said coolly, making no attempt to hide the paperwork she had spread out across the marquetry of the secretaire.

The young man looked down at the documents, his moustache curling with contempt, like a leech on a hot-plate. "I see you have discovered my father's little secret," he said (in French, of course).

"Yes. And I think he's playing the worst kind of thimble-jiggler's trick. In England, we have a tradition of fair play, in sport as in everything else. You'd never find an Englishman doing something as banana-shaped as this."

"No, it is not good," said Florian. "Often Papa goes too far."

Twinks looked at him in amazement. She had been expecting him to defend his father's double-dealing; instead, he actually seemed to be agreeing with her.

"You mean you do not approve of what the four-faced filcher is doing?"

"No, of course I do not! Like him, of course, I wish to win the Great Road Race. But I wish to win by my own merit as a driver. I do not wish cheating practices to be employed to ensure my victory. The Florian is a splendid piece of engineering. It would win the race anyway." Twinks had her own views on that matter, but she didn't say anything. "I do not like to be given an advantage over the other drivers by the wickedness of my father."

"Are you saying your Pater's wicked?" asked Twinks in astonishment.

"Yes. He is a man without honour. How I wish I had been brought up to abide by the principles of fair play, like your splendid brother Devereux Lyminster. I am frequently ashamed to be part of the Carré-Dagneau family."

This was all so unexpected that Twinks couldn't help pointing out: "On the previous occasions that we have met, you have not behaved as if you were ashamed of your family. You've spent all your time running the Carré-Dagneau banner up your flagpole and saluting it."

"And why do you think that is, Honoria?"

"I haven't got a mousesqueak of an idea."

"It is because, every other time you have seen me, Papa has been present. He is a cruel man. If he hears me voice even the tiniest criticism of him or the way he runs Les Automobiles Carré-Dagneau, then he will make life hell for me."

"Well, Madeira cake crumbs!" said Twinks in surprise. Now, she was the last person in the world to be described as gullible. Indeed, she had detected duplicity beneath a veneer of sincerity in many continents. But something in what Florian had said struck a chord with her. She thought how differently she behaved when she was in the presence of the Dowager Duchess. The Mater was a figure of such crushing authority that Twinks frequently had to curb her instinctively independent thoughts in the old woman's presence. It was only when she was away from such malign influence that she could truly be herself. So, she recognised the possibility of truth in what Florian Carré-Dagneau had said. And decided, at least for the time being, to give him the benefit of the doubt.

"Oh, the way Papa behaves makes me so angry!" Florian suddenly flared up. "But I must never alienate him. If I cross Papa, he will see to it that I do not inherit the company. And that is something I must do."

"You want to ensure you have as much of the old jingle-jangle as your father does — is that it?"

"No, the money is irrelevant. But to take over the company is my destiny. My wish, when I am Directeur Général, is to make Les Automobiles Carré-Dagneau a by-word for honest business practices. My ambition, as well as creating wonderful cars, is to introduce better working conditions for the company's employees, and to use my wealth in charitable ways to help the poor and distressed."

"You are so different from how you appeared before," said Twinks. "The zebra really has scrubbed off its stripes. At dinner you were behaving like another spoilt bratling, thinking he could exercise his *droit de seigneur* over any woman who tickled his taste buds." Fortunately, perhaps, Blotto wasn't there to wonder what the French for *droit de seigneur* was.

"No, no, I am not such a bounder! Again, because my father was in the room, I was behaving as he expects me to behave. I do not enjoy playing the cad, but I cannot break the hold my father has over me." Florian's face became more serious. "If you wish, to show I am really on the side of good, I could show you even more evidence of his misdeeds."

"Oh?"

"There is a secret room below this study, in what used to be the château's dungeon. It is there that my father keeps the files detailing the system of bribery and corruption by which he has always run Les Automobiles Carré-Dagneau. Would you like to see these files?"

"Would I? Give that pony a rosette!"

"Then I will show you."

Florian Carré-Dagneau moved towards the wall behind the secretaire. He took hold of a carved wooden *fleur-de-lys* and gave it a sharp twist. Immediately, a wall panel slid back, to reveal an old stone staircase leading downwards. Florian flicked a switch to illuminate the passageway. "Follow me, and you will see the proofs of serious crime."

"Splendissimo!" said Twinks, stepping down on to the staircase as the wall panel automatically slid across behind them.

Scarcely had that panel closed before another on the opposite wall opened. Giselle ushered Blotto into the study and closed the metal gate of the lift. Rather confused, he asked, "Is this where you show me your inner sanctum?"

"No, here what we have is the inner sanctum of my father."

"Is it, by Denzil?" said Blotto. His confusion increased. He had been assuming that an inner sanctum was a part of the female anatomy, but now it seemed that Jean-Marie Carré-Dagneau had one too. Blotto was confronted by the possibility that he himself might also be the possessor of an inner sanctum. He didn't know. Boys had been taught absolutely nothing about their bodies at Eton. Knowledge of that kind could, in the school's view, only lead to trouble.

"No, for what I have to show you, we need to go further down." And Giselle reached for the wooden *fleur-de-lys* on the wall.

Twinks turned at the sound of footsteps on the stone stairs, but Florian showed no surprise. He had been expecting the new arrivals.

The space in which Blotto found himself — just as his sister had minutes before — was stone-built and apparently windowless. Water and slime glinted on the walls. There was a foetid smell of mud and sewage. A gate of metal railings had been pushed back against the wall by the entrance to the staircase. Fixed to the stone floor were rusty chains, which confirmed the room had in the past been used as a dungeon. It was painful to contemplate the fate of those who had once been attached to the chains.

As the Carré-Dagneaux siblings leapt towards the stairs and clanged the metal door shut behind them, Blotto and Twinks realised that the place could still be used as a dungeon. Triumphant French laughter rubbed that message in.

As did the shouted words of the departing Florian Carré-Dagneau. "You have no hope! No one has ever escaped from the dungeon of the Château d'Igeaux! And, as for thoughts of being set free by some charitable soul, put them from your mind! No one will attempt to release you, because no one knows you are here!"

Twinks felt furious with herself. She should never have believed Florian's words about behaving differently when his father was not present. The two Carré-Dagneaux were as bad as each other. Father and son were cut from the same duplicitous cloth.

Both she and Blotto had been far too easily tricked. For him, she didn't mind. Her brother's passage through life had always been something of a Gullible's Travels. But that she herself had fallen for such a simple deception . . . Twinks seethed with anger.

CHAPTER
THIRTEEN

Corky Uses His Loaf

Maybe it was the sound of the Lagonda's passenger door closing that made Corky Froggett stir from his deep sleep. He was too late and too bleary to see who had closed it, but the evidence of a recent visitor lay on the passenger seat. The first smell he received was one of coffee, the second of fresh bread. He looked across to see a low wide cup of *café au lait*, next to a basket containing a fresh *baguette*, a dish of butter and a small pot of apricot jam.

He wondered if his breakfast benefactor was the delightfully Yvette-shaped woman in the maid's uniform who had promised him dinner (and so much more) the previous evening.

Suddenly aware how hungry and thirsty he was, Corky took a long restorative swallow of coffee, before breaking off a length of *baguette* and lavishly buttering and jamming it. He was halfway down the bread before he thought to look outside the car.

And then he realised, with a sickening impact, that the Lagonda was the only vehicle in the courtyard of Château d'Igeaux.

Nor was there any sign of the Young Master and the Young Mistress.

He took his watch out of his uniform pocket and saw with horror that it was just gone eight thirty.

The other competitors in the Great Road Race (not to mention the adult Carré-Dagneaux in their Adélaïde) had departed without the Lagonda team, and now had half an hour's lead!

The staff he questioned inside the château had not seen the English siblings and had no idea where they might be. Whether this was actually true, or whether they were saying what Jean-Marie Carré-Dagneau had told them to say didn't really matter. Clearly, Corky was not going to get any help from them in his search.

Still clutching the remains of his *baguette*, Corky Froggett decided that this last dereliction of his duty was unforgivable. In the past he had on occasion let down the Young Master and the Young Mistress, though never on this scale. And usually he had been able to find a way of making it up to them. But to have fallen asleep when his obvious duty had been to guard the Lagonda all night cast him out into some hitherto uncharted circle of hell.

Not only had he failed to guard the Lagonda, he had also failed to protect his employers. He felt certain that they had met their fate on his watch. Quite what form that fate had been he did not know but, given the record of criminality he had witnessed from the Carré-Dagneau family, Corky feared the worst. Crécy and Agincourt had been avenged. Devereux and

Honoria Lyminster, he felt certain, had been done away with by the perfidious French. And he was the one person who might possibly have saved them from an ignominious death.

Corky had no alternative. It had always been his ambition to lay down his life for the Lyminster family, and now at last the moment had arrived. He would have preferred to have died in battle than to take his own life, but extreme situations demanded extreme measures. It was the only way he could atone for his appalling lapse of the night before.

He knew where he would do the deed. Still holding the unnoticed remains of his *baguette*, he set off towards the moat of Château d'Igeaux.

Down in the château's dungeon, Twinks had spent a frustrating night trying to find a way out of the gluepot in which she and Blotto had found themselves. She also taxed her brain with the big questions prompted by the letter she had found in Jean-Marie Carré-Dagneau's study. Who had it been addressed to? And what was the "organisation" he referred to?

While her brother slept, she used the electric torch from her sequinned reticule to examine every square inch of the dungeon, probing for any weakness in its stone structure. But the medieval builders had done a good, tight job. (Twinks, whose knowledge of architecture matched her knowledge of everything else, recognised that, though the main château had been built in the Renaissance period, the dungeon dated from much earlier.) They had left no chinks in their closely fitted stonework and, since the space was underground, removing one of the blocks would only offer the prospect of inundation or weeks of tunnelling.

Apart from the gate to the staircase, whose massive locks Twinks had inspected, coming to the sad conclusion that they were too strong even for the sophisticated picklocks in her sequinned reticule, the only other opening in the dungeon was a narrow slot at the top of the wall. This was protected by metal bars too close to allow even someone as slender as Twinks to slip through. The concentration of staining and slime down the wall beneath this aperture suggested that it probably opened out on to the moat.

Inspection with the periscope that she produced from her sequinned reticule confirmed this conjecture. And when she climbed up the collapsible ladder (which she also kept in her sequinned reticule) for a closer look, she found she was indeed looking out on to the surface of the moat. But the pale moon was behind clouds and the beam of her torch did not reach far enough to see the other side. She would have to wait till daylight to see if there was any escape route that way.

She wasn't optimistic. Which was unusual for Twinks. Though infinitely more intelligent than her brother, she normally shared his sunny view of the world and everything in it. But the dungeon of Château d'Igeaux had dampened even her customary ebullience.

When she was at the top of the collapsible ladder, she tested the strength of the bars which shut them off from freedom. Though discoloured and flaking, they had only been affected by rust on the surface. The centre of the metal rods remained strong and, planted deeply into the stone above and beneath, immovable.

Disconsolately, Twinks went back down the collapsible ladder. She collapsed it and returned it to her sequinned reticule. Then she lay down on the stone floor of the dungeon and experienced a few moments of fitful sleep. It was hard to decide whether her dreams or the realities she kept awaking to were the more dispiriting.

Once Corky Froggett had made a decision, he was the kind of man who stood by it. As he walked across the courtyard of the Château d'Igeaux, he went towards the Lagonda and gave the splendid monster's long blue bonnet an emotional stroke of farewell. He regretted that his last view of the worshipped vehicle would be with it bearing a red and white pennant advertising the products of Les Automobiles Carré-Dagneau.

Then he bent down to pick up gravel and fill his uniform pockets with it. He set off through the main gates to find the moat.

Twinks's disjointed sleep must have given way, from sheer exhaustion, to something more settled, because she was annoyed to wake up, stiff on the cold floor, to find from the watch in her sequinned reticule that it was after eight thirty. The other side of the dungeon, Blotto snored on. It took more than the prospect of starving to death in a French prison to put him off his sleep.

Twinks contemplated shouting for help but, knowing that the dungeon was shut off from the rest of the château by vast thicknesses of stone, decided not to bother. She had tried immediately after they had been incarcerated the night before and been rewarded only by the echo of the dungeon's vast emptiness.

So, instead of calling for help, she reassembled her collapsible ladder to see if the view from the moat-side grille offered any more hopeful prospects in the daylight.

Corky Froggett stood by the moat, looking up at the ornate building in front of him, and thought his last thoughts. As he did so, he became aware that he was still holding the half-*baguette*. At the same moment, he noticed a pair of ducks swimming by the château wall.

To end his life on an act of kindness appealed to some charitable instinct within his wizened psyche. Crumbling the bread in his hands, he tossed pieces towards the ducks, who were sporting themselves by a low, narrow grille, set only just above the water level. The shadow cast by the sun prevented him from seeing anything beyond the bars.

As one of the ducks pounced on the bread, the other one quacked, and through the quack, Corky heard a strange, echoey voice say, "You have saved us, Corky!"

Unused to being addressed by ducks, the chauffeur was a little perplexed. "Well, I just gave you a bit of bread. I —" he started, but the duck cut him off.

"Whatever you were about to do, Corky, do not do it!"

He was in a quandary. Having made the decision to end his life, he really ought to go through with it. On the other hand, being told not to by a strange, echoey voice was quite a powerful message to receive.

"What you must do," the duck went on, "is rescue us."

"Why, what's wrong with you? You look perfectly happy, swimming around."

"No, you must rescue Blotto and Twinks!"

"That would be better than laying down my life for them?"

"Much better." And the duck gave him instructions as to how to get into the study of Jean-Marie Carré-Dagneau, and which *fleur-de-lys* on the wall should be turned to access the secret staircase.

"I will do it straight away," he said.

Not a man to believe in the spirit world or divine intervention, the chauffeur was still aware that he had undergone some kind of life-changing psychic experience.

Corky Froggett had never really believed in God. But now he did not rule out the possibility of believing in ducks.

CHAPTER
FOURTEEN

Nastiness on Narrow Roads

"Splendissimo!" said Twinks, as the Lagonda wolfed down the open road towards Lyon. The top was down, the sun was shining and the countryside looking absolutely beautiful (even though it was French). "All's right with the world!" she cried, knowing that she was quoting Robert Browning.

"Tickey-Tockey!" said Blotto, unaware that she was quoting anything.

The only thing, of course, that was wrong with their world was that they had left the Château d'Igeaux at nine minutes and four seconds past nine. Which, added to their three minutes and twenty seconds deficit of the day before, meant they were starting one hour, twelve minutes and twenty-four seconds after the other competitors.

But neither Blotto nor Twinks mentioned this potentially dispiriting fact. They were both confident that his driving and her navigational skills would see them soon back in contention. Better than in contention — back in the lead.

Behind them in the car, Corky Froggett's eyes were closed. But he wasn't asleep. The remaining bits of gravel in his pockets reminded him that he'd recently undergone a life-changing experience. Even though, when he had rescued his employers from the dungeon, Twinks had assured him it was her voice he'd heard from behind the ducks, he wasn't convinced. That echoey sound had been something beyond human. As a result, his mind was all confusion. Though the chauffeur had undergone many hardships and privations in his life, he had never before had a spiritual crisis. And it hit him hard. One question kept resonating through his mind. Should he give up everything he believed in — cars, protecting the Young Master and the Young Mistress, and shooting people — to devote the rest of his life to the worship of ducks?

The Lagonda swept through Lyon and, though they had no means of knowing for sure, Blotto, Twinks and Corky felt certain that they were gaining on the other cars. The shameful idea that they might not win the Great Road Race did not enter their heads. One hour, twelve minutes and twenty-four seconds could easily be made up.

It was just outside Valence that they hit a problem. Very nearly did hit it, too. They were going so fast that the Lagonda almost crashed into the roadblock. As they came to a juddering, dusty halt only inches from the wooden barriers, an officious-looking uniformed gendarme detached himself from a group of his colleagues and came towards them, shaking an admonitory finger.

"You are driving dangerously fast," he told the driver.

Since this was said in French, Blotto, having no idea what he meant, nodded cheerfully and said, "Good ticket."

Twinks, meanwhile, engaged the gendarme in his own language. "What is the meaning of this delay?" she asked with an *hauteur* of which Marie Antoinette would not have been ashamed.

"The road is blocked, mademoiselle," he replied with appropriate deference.

"I can see that," said Twinks, now doing a convincing impression of the Dowager Duchess. "But *why* is it blocked?"

"There is an obstacle on the road ahead."

"What kind of obstacle?"

"An obstacle which has necessitated our building this roadblock," he replied unhelpfully.

Twinks changed tack. "And how long is this roadblock likely to stay in place?"

"Certainly until the end of the day."

"How do you know that?"

"Because those are the instructions I have been given."

"And who gave you those instructions?" asked Twinks, who thought the Carré-Dagneaux were quite capable of setting up the obstacle.

"My superiors," the gendarme replied, again unhelpfully. "The recommended diversion is via Grenoble."

134

"I think I can find a better diversion than that," came the icy reply from Twinks, who had, needless to say, memorised the entire road map of France. "And tell me, man . . ." She knew the French had abolished their aristocracy, but that wasn't going to stop her from giving them a dose of hers ". . . have you seen any other cars this morning, bearing a red and white pennant like the one on our bonnet?"

"I have seen three. One of the drivers appeared to be Italian, one American, and the third German."

"And did they pass through the barrier?"

"Of course they did not."

"So you've diverted them via Grenoble?"

"That was the route I advised them to take, yes."

"And those are the only cars with this pennant that you saw?" The gendarme's silence was long enough to raise Twinks's suspicion. She pounced on the hesitation. "You didn't see a purple car called a Florian, manufactured by Les Automobiles Carré-Dagneau?"

Again, the gendarme was silent for too long.

"Tell me! What happened to the Florian?" Twinks demanded imperiously.

"It passed through here earlier," he admitted.

"Earlier? Before the roadblock was in place?"

"Yes, mademoiselle."

The four-faced filchers! thought Twinks in high fury. She felt certain that the Carré-Dagneau family had bribed the gendarmerie to let Florian through and divert the other competitors. Finding the money would not have been a problem for them. Was there any perfidy to which they would not stoop?

$\star$ $\star$ $\star$

Driving all the way to Grenoble would not only add many miles to their journey, it would also take them into much more difficult terrain. From Lyon, the Lagonda had basically been following the valley of the Rhône, a relatively flat passage between the Massif Central and the Alps. Moving east from Valence would take them into more mountainous country.

Rather than reducing their one hour, twelve minutes and twenty-four second deficit, they would definitely be adding to it. The knowledge that Enrico Parmigiano-Reggiano, Brad Gimlet and Count Daspoontz would be suffering the same handicap was small comfort, given that they knew Florian Carré-Dagneau had swanned through Valence on the main road towards Avignon.

But now Twinks's map-memorising skills came into their own. Because of the blockage at Valence, there was a lot of traffic on the roads east, but she found a quicker route through minor lanes and tiny villages, where the speeding Lagonda created its customary mayhem, skittling the peasantry.

Her efforts were rewarded when, about half an hour out of Valence, breasting the top of a mountain, they saw, on the switchback road below them, Brad Gimlet's Cadebaker, closely followed by Count Daspoontz's Krumpfenbach. Twinks's shorter route, possibly aided by longer delays at the Valence roadblock, had reduced the time between them to less than ten minutes.

Where Enrico Parmigiano-Reggiano's Fettuccine roadster was, they had no idea. But it too must have had to take the diverted route, so the team in the

136

Lagonda felt encouraged that the Italians could not be too far ahead. In spite of the tight curves of the narrow road and the vertiginous drop to the right-hand side, Blotto pressed down harder on the accelerator. With each bend of the switchback, they had to turn the other way to see what was happening with the two cars on the road below.

And there was no doubt that the Germans were gaining on the Americans. At each twist of their lower part of the switchback, the great nose of the Krumpfenbach drew closer to the rear of the Cadebaker, though the narrowness of the road meant that Count Daspoontz would have to wait to overtake until they were on a broader stretch.

Or perhaps it should be said that a more scrupulous driver would have waited to overtake. The Count clearly had no time for such niceties. To the horror of the three watchers in the Lagonda, he suddenly found extra power, shot the Krumpfenbach Big Eight hard into the back of the vehicle in front and pushed the Cadebaker off the road, through a flimsy wooden barrier, and out of sight into the ravine below.

The German team clearly had no intention of stopping to give assistance to their displaced rivals. With a triumphant fanfare on its horn, the huge Krumpfenbach sped along the open road ahead. "The spoffing stenchers!" cried Blotto, urging the Lagonda on at greater speed towards the scene of the crime.

The thought of not stopping to help did not occur to anyone in the Lagonda. It wasn't only the Battle of Waterloo that had been won on the playing fields of

Eton, it was also there that Blotto's natural sense of fair play had been refined. For an English gentleman, helping his fellow man was always going to have priority over winning any Great Road Race — or repairing the Tawcester Towers plumbing.

He brought the Lagonda to a halt beside the broken railing, leapt out of the car and looked down the mountainside, preparing himself for the worst. Twinks and Corky stood at either side.

The Cadebaker had skittered some hundred yards down the ravine, ripping up scrubby trees and other vegetation that grew in its way. It had come to rest when its front fender met a rocky outcrop. From the way the car lay, the impact seemed to have broken both axles and possibly done even more devastating damage to the chassis.

But the damage to the machine didn't concern Blotto. He was more worried about its occupants and immediately started in a stumbling run down the hillside.

Before he reached the Cadebaker, he was relieved to see Brad Gimlet emerge from it, dusty and in shock, but otherwise apparently able to move all right. The only visible damage was the wide gap where his parade of beautiful teeth had smashed into the steering wheel.

The two mechanics in their stars-and-stripes overalls, however, had not fared so well. The one in the back seat couldn't put any weight on his right leg, and the one in the front, whose forehead had shattered its way through the windscreen, was unconscious.

138

"We need to get these poor thimbles to a hospital," said Blotto. Turning to Twinks, who had just arrived by the Cadebaker and who he knew would have the answer, he asked, "Where is the nearest bone-setting bureau?"

"One in Grenoble, one in Valence," she replied instantly. "The Valence one's a couple of hours closer. We passed it just before we hit the roadblock."

"Then we pongle our way back to Valence," announced Blotto, without a moment's hesitation.

It took a while to get the injured up the mountainside and into the Lagonda. Then Blotto turned the car round and, driving more cautiously to avoid shaking up the patients in the back, he made his way back to Valence.

Not only for the Americans, but also for the English team, the Great Road Race was over.

CHAPTER
FIFTEEN

Mischief in Monaco

Though they had remained outwardly positive on the drive back, once they had delivered the three Americans into the safe hands of the Valence hospital nurses, Blotto, Twinks and Corky could no longer sustain their cheerfulness.

"It really has put lumps in the custard," said Blotto mournfully, as they walked back to the Lagonda.

"And pitched the crud into the crumpet," Twinks agreed.

"It's a bloomin' shame, that's what it is," Corky contributed.

"Well, we're not going to need this any more, that's for sure," said Blotto, tearing the Les Automobiles Carré-Dagneau pennant off his precious car. "I never liked my Lag being a billboard for those lumps of toadspawn, anyway."

"No," Twinks agreed, as they got in, Corky once again in the back. "Oh, we're really both feet in the quagmire! I just feel such a bonebrain for having fallen for Florian Carré-Dagneau's wheedling words. I should have realised he was just full of meringue. Once a stencher, always a stencher."

"Don't blame yourself, sis. I swallowed Giselle's artificial fly just as easily. When she said she was a *femme fatale*, I should have realised there was something fishy."

"Why?"

"Because a *femme* is some kind of fish, isn't it? You know, when you have *sole bonne femme*, you —"

"Don't don your worry-boots about it, Blotters. You're just too trusting. You think it's beyond the barbed wire to be suspicious of a lady . . ."

"Well, I —"

"Which means you're a sap for anything that makes a moue at you."

"A 'moue'?" He was surprised by his sister's uncharacteristic impoliteness. "Twinks me old shaving brush, it's way beyond the rule book to call Giselle Carré-Dagneau a cow."

"I didn't mean that kind of 'moo'."

"Sorry, not on the same page?"

"A 'moue' is a kind of pout at which Frenchwomen are remarkably adept and — oh, forget it, Blotters."

Silence descended on the interior of the Lagonda.

Blotto broke it by asking mournfully, "So, what do we do now?" Even in his customary sunny mood, he always let his sister make decisions of that kind. Or any kind, come to that.

"I suppose we see if we can get into Valence, find a half-decent hotel, and have as good a dinner as we can get, with lots of the old alkiboodles. Then, in the morning, we get on the turntable and set course back for Tawcester Towers."

"Tickey-Tockey," agreed a very subdued Blotto. "Oh, this really is the flea's armpit!"

Another silence in the Lagonda told him that neither of his companions had anything to add to this assessment of the situation. Twinks's mind was racing. She thought back to the carbon of the letter she had seen in Jean-Marie Carré-Dagneau's study, which had ordered sabotage of the Florian's rivals. Now, having witnessed the crime on the mountainside, she wondered whether the instructions had been given to the Germans. Were they doing the Carré-Dagneaux's dirty work for them? And once again, the question rose to the surface of her mind: what on earth was the "organisation" referred to in the letter?

"Of course," said Corky Froggett lugubriously, "if the roadblock's still in place we won't be able to get into Valence to find a hotel, anyway. That copper in the poncy uniform said this morning that it would be in place for the rest of the day."

Blotto groaned. "So, we might as well turn straight round and start back for Blighty now."

"Rein in the roans there," said Twinks. "Let's just check the roadblock still is in place first."

When they reached the site where it had been, there was no sign of any roadblock. No sign it had ever been there. And that was the first indication that their luck might be changing.

They drove on, following the main road, knowing that Count Daspoontz's Krumpfenbach Big Eight and Enrico Parmigiano-Reggiano's Fettuccine roadster were both travelling on a lengthy diversion via

Grenoble. Florian Carré-Dagneau in his Florian was probably by now a long way ahead of them, but he was the only one who was. It was a cheering thought.

Twinks's navigational skills cut off the odd corner on their route from Avignon to Monaco and reduced their time deficit by a few minutes. The check-in point for the end of the day's leg was outside the main entrance to the Hôtel Huge in Monte Carlo. And you couldn't miss it. The whole area was draped with red and white banners promoting Les Automobiles Carré-Dagneau.

Adélaïde Carré-Dagneau sat indolently at a table under the wide glass canopy. A bottle of champagne lolled in an ice bucket in front of her and she sipped at her glass with the *insouciance* of someone who didn't expect to have her idyll broken into in the near future. Twinks was amused by the sudden change of expression that the sight of the Lagonda forced on to the woman's face.

But of course, Adélaïde Carré-Dagneau couldn't say anything. To admit any level of surprise at their arrival would be a virtual admission that she knew her children had imprisoned Blotto and Twinks in the Château d'Igeaux dungeon. So, she just meekly made a note of their time of arrival in her ledger.

Twinks checked what had actually been written down. Events of the last few days ruled out the possibility of her trusting anything the Carré-Dagneaux did.

"Presumably, your apology of a son in the Florian has already checked in?" she asked.

"Yes," the proud mother replied smugly. She pointed across the road to where the violet Florian was parked against a perfect Mediterranean backdrop. Then she checked the figures she had written down, looked at her watch and said, "He is two hours, twelve minutes and forty-three seconds ahead of you."

Twinks looked at her brother, whose mouth had opened to unleash a stream of invective about the differences between English and French attitudes when it came to fair play, and shook her head. Blotto obediently closed his mouth.

Having had their luggage collected by a hotel porter, Blotto and Twinks checked in. Corky Froggett parked the Lagonda some five yards behind the Florian.

The dinner they enjoyed in the hotel restaurant was excellent. The main course was fish which, after he had scraped all the frenchified sauce off it, Blotto found very toothsome. In defiance of protocol, he had insisted that Corky should dine with them.

The chauffeur was silent over the meal. Whether that was because the food reminded him of the lost Yvette, or he was distracted by his spiritual search for the true ducks and worried by the appearance of ducks in a variety of sauces on the menu, it was impossible to know.

Because summer had come early that year, the hotel's restaurant terrace was open and, as Blotto and Twinks sat in the balmy twilight, eating splendid food and drinking fine wines, they felt more cheerful than they had since they arrived in France.

They looked down from their splendid viewpoint to the lights of the promenade and the darkening sea beyond. On the road opposite were parked the competing cars in the Great Road Race, in order of arrival in Monte Carlo. There were gaps of some five yards between them, generous space allowing access for the teams' mechanics to perform any necessary engine-tuning.

First in the line-up, of course, was the Florian, next the Lagonda, then the Fettuccine roadster. Fourth was the Krumpfenbach Big Eight. It was a source of satisfaction to Blotto and Twinks that the Italians had beaten the Germans, but they could not dismiss from their minds the violence with which they had seen Count Daspoontz remove his American opposition. So they didn't argue when Corky Froggett insisted that he would once again spend the night in the Lagonda to prevent further foul play. And, though they thought he was being overcautious, they fully understood why he refused to touch any of the Hôtel Huge's fine wines, in case they were drugged.

Since their arrival, the English team hadn't seen any of the other competitors but, as they were enjoying an excellent post-prandial Armagnac, they were surprised to see Count Daspoontz enter the restaurant and come straight towards their table.

"Zo," he said, "ve hav ze same timinks. Ve are . . . how you say? Throat and throat?"

"Neck and neck," suggested Twinks.

"Sorry, not on the same page?" said Blotto.

"Our timinks are ze same," said the Count. "Ve vere diverted by a false roadblock at Valence vich you managed to avoid."

Blotto was about to explain to the German, in no uncertain terms, that they had also been delayed by the roadblock, and also by taking to hospital the Americans who had been deliberately injured by the Krumpfenbach Big Eight. But, not for the first time, an admonitory shake of the head from his sister made him hold his tongue.

"But," Count Daspoontz continued, "my excellent driving means ve caught up viz you in terms of time. Tomorrow ve start on ze level playing field."

Blotto curbed the expression of his view that the German team wouldn't recognise a level playing field if it jumped up and bit them on the knee. Instead, he just said, "May the best man win."

"Oh, the best man will win," announced a French-accented voice. A very smug-looking Florian Carré-Dagneau had suddenly appeared by the table. "And we all know who that will be. The best man between you two, the English and the German, will be the one who comes second."

Blotto looked across at Twinks, but her azure eyes again deterred him from rising to the provocation. It pained him not to respond in kind, but he contented himself with a feeble, "Well, we'll see what happens tomorrow."

"Oh yes, we will," Florian agreed, before drifting away on an infuriating giggle.

"Till tomorrow zen!" Count Daspoontz screwed in his monocle, clicked his heels together and bowed, before also leaving them to their Armagnac.

"The out-of-bounders!" Blotto seethed. "Why didn't you let me give them a prick of their own poison?"

"Because," Twinks replied coolly, "nothing infuriates showoffs like that more than getting no response. We will defeat the slugbuckets by our actions rather than our words."

"Good ticket," said Blotto.

They were surprised at that moment to be joined by Enrico Parmigiano-Reggiano. Since first being introduced to him, they had exchanged no more than a few words and so had not expected to be addressed in near-perfect English.

"I thought," he said, "as we near the climax of the Great Road Race, we might benefit from pooling our experience of the consistent pattern of sabotage which has been going on."

"You've spotted a bit of under-the-counter diddling too, have you?" asked Blotto.

"It would be hard to miss it."

Twinks was cautious about the new arrival. Her experiences up to that point in the Great Road Race had made her wary of trusting anyone. And in the Italian's case, she could not forget the vulgar gestures he had made to Ronald the Second Mechanic on the roadside in Dover. Seeing him close to, though, she could not deny that he had a swarthy Latin allure. Then again, Italians had a long history of corruption and double-dealing. Still, she was interested to find out more about Enrico Parmigiano-Reggiano. Gesturing to a waiter to bring another chair, she said, "Please park your knees under our tablecloth."

"With pleasure, *signorina*," said the Italian, with a facial expression that Blotto recognised all too well. He had seen many men, on first looking closely at his sister, take on the look of a poleaxed puppy.

In the hopes of stopping Enrico from actually drooling, Blotto asked, "Have the stenchers crocked your car?"

"No. Or perhaps I should say 'not yet'. I don't trust them a centimetre." He looked down at the parked vehicles. "I don't see the Americans' car there. When I last saw them, they were just behind us. Have they been sabotaged by the Carré-Dagneaux too?"

"You're bong on the nose that they've been sabotaged. But the slugbuckets who did it weren't the Frenchies." And Blotto proceeded to describe the crime they had witnessed on the mountain road towards Grenoble.

At the end of the narrative, Enrico Parmigiano-Reggiano looked thoughtful. "So, it's not just the Carré-Dagneaux we have to watch out for. Oh, and by the way, there's still no sign of your compatriot, the one in the Bentley."

"Trumbo McCorquodash?"

"That's the one. Who sabotaged him — the French or the Germans?"

Twinks grinned. "I think that could be a case of self-sabotage."

"Oh?"

"Trumbo is a bit of a mouth-magnet for French wine. The idea that he drove his Ben through the

Rhône Valley without visiting a few vineyards just doesn't pass as possible."

"Oh well, that's a relief," said Parmigiano-Reggiano. "Do you reckon that roadblock at Valence was the Carré-Dagneaux's doing?"

"As sure as a newt's amphibious," said Twinks. "And what proves it is that that moustachioed squiffball Florian in his Florian was allowed through before the roadblock was set up."

The Italian growled with annoyance. "They'll do anything to stop anyone else winning. I sometimes think the whole Great Road Race was set up as a publicity stunt for Les Automobiles Carré-Dagneau."

"Give that pony a rosette!" said Twinks. And she told him about the posters and documents she'd found in the Château d'Igeaux.

"So, what kind of lead has Florian got now?" asked the Italian.

"Two hours, twelve minutes and forty-three seconds," came the reply from Blotto. "Mind you, the Lag'll reel that in in no time."

Enrico Parmigiano-Reggiano looked dubious. "It's a lot, and there's not much open road for overtaking between here and Rome."

"Don't worry. I'll bring home the banco," said Blotto, with instinctive confidence.

The Italian rubbed his chin thoughtfully. "I think maybe some sabotage should be directed towards the Florian . . ."

Blotto was offended. "Now rein in the roans there! Are you suggesting that we should sink to such rat-wrangling?"

"No, no."

"If not us, then who? Surely you wouldn't stoop to that kind of mud-meddling?"

"No. But, after what he did to the Cadebaker, it sounds as if Count Daspoontz will do anything to win. I might pass on a few suggestions to him of ways to get the Florian out of contention. That way we might cancel out both the French and the German and make the Great Road Race a straight duel between your Lagonda and my Fettuccine roadster."

"Good ticket!" said Blotto, lost in admiration.

"Splendissimo!" murmured Twinks, and Parmigiano-Reggiano glowed in the warmth of her commendation.

Still smiling, he said, "From that letter you saw at the Château d'Igeaux, it sounds as though the thought of anyone else winning hasn't occurred to Jean-Marie Carré-Dagneau."

"No, the filcher's convinced he'll be handing over the chest of sovs to his son, who will presumably hand them back to his Papa at a later mo."

"But if someone else does cross the winning line at the Colosseum, he'll have to hand the prize money over to them, won't he?"

"If he gets as much press there in Rome for the final whistle as he did for the bully-off in Trafalgar Square, there's no way he can avoid it."

"You're right." Parmigiano-Reggiano nodded. "But if he does hand the sovereigns to someone else, he's quite capable of trying to steal them back from the winner."

"He spoffing well won't be able to do that if the Lag's first over the line," asserted Blotto.

150

"How can you be so sure?"

"Because, for a start, we'll have our chauffeur guarding the hoard like a cat over a mousehole."

Hearing this reference to himself, Corky Froggett came out of a reverie about the divinity of ducks and endorsed the Young Master's statement.

"Nobody will steal from the Lag while I'm around. I'll stop them, even if I have to do it with my dead body!"

"Also," Blotto went on, "even if those Carré-Dagneau lumps of toadspawn get past Corky . . ."

"Which they won't, milord."

"No, of course they won't — never in a nun's wedding night! But if they do, they won't find the chest of sovs, anyway."

"Why not?"

"Because they'll be hidden in a secret place!"

"Well, that's int —"

But Enrico Parmigiano-Reggiano did not say any more, because at that moment there was a loud bang and a flash of a fireball. The four of them looked out towards the sea, in shock at the sight of the Italian's Fettuccine roadster engulfed in flames.

CHAPTER
SIXTEEN

Corky Looks for Evidence

The Fettuccine roadster was almost completely destroyed. The Hôtel Huge porters had rushed out with hoses to extinguish the flames. Now steam mingled with smoke from the heap of blackened and twisted metal.

Because of the distance between the parked cars, there was minimal damage to the two nearest, the Lagonda and the Krumpfenbach Big Eight, from which shreds of burning debris were quickly brushed off.

Blotto, Twinks and Corky stood on the seaside promenade, looking on as Enrico Parmigiano-Reggiano surveyed the ruins of his shattered motoring dreams. Watching from the hotel entrance were all four Carré-Dagneaux. Sympathetically, Blotto said to the Italian, "Bit of a candle-snuffer, isn't it, me old greengage? What do you reckon? Mechanical failure? Engine overheated?"

"No." Enrico pointed to a set of tangled wires visible through the smoke. "It was a bomb. Deliberate sabotage."

"Well, I'll be kippered like a herring! But we had our peepers clapped on the cars from the restaurant terrace. We'd have seen any running sore who fixed a bomb under your Fettuccine."

"It wasn't fixed here in Monte Carlo." Parmigiano-Reggiano gestured towards a discoloured clock-face amidst the smoking detritus. "It was on a timing device. Probably planted and set in motion last night at Château d'Igeaux ... by someone who didn't care whether the bomb went off while there was anyone in the car or not. In other words, someone who didn't care whether I and my mechanics survived or not."

"Well, I'll be battered like a pudding!" said Blotto, shocked at the levels of criminality to which humankind can sink. "You could have all been coffinated!"

"Only too easily."

"What kind of sewer rat would put a bomb in a boddo's car?"

Parmigiano-Reggiano looked towards the Krumpfenbach. "Maybe the kind of sewer rat who'd knock another car down a mountainside ...?"

Twinks looked towards the Carré-Dagneau family. "Or maybe the kind of sewer rat who would bribe the gendarmerie to set up an unnecessary roadblock ...?"

"Anyway," said Enrico Parmigiano-Reggiano with grim resolution, "this is a declaration of war! They asked for it, and they are going to get it! When I find out which of these two twisters has caused this, they will find out that two can play at the sabotage game!"

"Only two?" asked Twinks.

"What do you mean?" When he looked at her, once again the Italian's jaw dropped into poleaxed puppy mode.

"You haven't included us, Enrico me old soap dish. We're as keen to win the Great Road Race as anyone else."

"As keen as mustard with Jereboams full of chillies in it!" asserted Blotto. "And don't doubt for a moment that we are going to win! What's two hours, twelve minutes and forty-three seconds, after all?"

The Italian smiled. "I do not include you in my list of suspects," he said, "because you are British. I trust you, and I am prepared to work with you to deal with the cheats in this competition. We will prove, I think, that the Great Road Race was, like many things, won on the playing fields of Eton."

"You're bong on the nose there!" said Blotto, regretting that he might, in the past, have been less than complimentary about the Italians. Now he came to think of it, they were really Grade A foundation stones . . . that is, considering they were foreign.

Twinks too was inclined to revise her opinion of Enrico Parmigiano-Reggiano. Having witnessed the violent sabotage to which his car had been subject, she was instantly less suspicious of him. And there was something rather attractive in his dark brown eyes.

Corky Froggett sat in the Lagonda and watched the moon shine down on its reflection in the deep blue of the Mediterranean. It was a magical and rather spiritual vision. He wondered for a moment whether he was about to witness a Manifestation of the Almighty Duck, but then reminded himself that they were freshwater rather than seawater birds. But they occupied his thoughts almost as much as machine-guns used to do.

Residual wisps of smoke still rose from the tangled wreckage of the Fettuccine roadster in front of him, and beyond that he could see the violet outline of the Florian. The sight filled him with impotent anger. He felt convinced that the Carré-Dagneaux were behind the bombing of the Italian car, and he longed to be able to produce proof that they had committed the crime. Achieving something like that would really put him in the good books of the Young Master and the Young Mistress.

He looked around. Most of the lights in the Hôtel Huge were out, and there was no one on the streets. If he did want to check out the Florian for evidence of wrongdoing, he would never have a better opportunity.

Corky Froggett slipped out of the Lagonda and moved silently, as he had learnt to do during the war, towards the French car. Clearly, its owners were not expecting any suspicious activity; they had not even locked it. He opened the driver's door and subjected the interior to detailed scrutiny.

Nothing. Or rather nothing that might serve as proof of guilt. Somewhat frustrated, he got out and moved round to the back. Rather than a dickey, the vehicle had a boot compartment for luggage. This too was unlocked. Corky lifted the lid and peered inside.

It was surprisingly capacious. And surprisingly empty. except for a metal cylinder whose purpose he could not identify. But in the far corner, the thin moonlight revealed a tangle of wires and other electrical

155

equipment. Feeling sure that these had something to do with the bomb's detonation system, Corky propped up the boot lid with a long spanner and leant forward.

But he couldn't reach. He'd have to get inside the compartment to secure his evidence. He climbed up on the sill of the boot and swung his legs inside.

Then, as his hand made contact with the wires, he heard the sound of his spanner prop slipping.

The lid of the boot clanged down and locked itself, imprisoning Corky Froggett inside.

CHAPTER
SEVENTEEN

The Full Monte Carlo

When Blotto and Twinks woke the next morning and looked out from the front of the Hôtel Huge, there was no sign that the Fettuccine roadster had ever been there. Not even a slick of oil or smoke discolouration on the white edging of the kerb bore witness to the destruction of the night before. Whether it was the civic authorities or the hotel staff who had done the clean-up, there was no means of knowing.

Nor was there evidence that there had been any police investigation into the planting of the bomb. Twinks immediately assumed that, once again, the right palms had been greased by the Carré-Dagneau family. Or possibly by Count Daspoontz and his team . . .? Their violence against the Americans had definitely moved them into her frame of suspicion.

So, the surviving participants in the Great Road Race ate a splendid and huge Full Monte Carlo Breakfast as though nothing untoward had happened. The only oddity encountered by Blotto and Twinks was the absence of Corky Froggett. From their vantage point in the restaurant, they could see no sign of him in the front seat of the Lagonda. Twinks was inclined to worry about where he might be, but Blotto reassured her that the chauffeur was no doubt, even as they spoke, downing a substantial breakfast in the hotel kitchen. "Boddoes like Corky never feel quite at ease eating with the Quality," he explained. "It's something to do with coming from generations of serfdom. Right and proper, really. It's fashionable these days to criticise the Feudal System, but it did get a lot of things right."

His sister, not entirely convinced, nodded.

Enrico Parmigiano-Reggiano was also in the restaurant, exchanging pleasantries with the French and German competitors, giving no sign of the revenge he was planning to visit upon one or other of them. Twinks was once again impressed by his Latin charm.

When the Italian stopped by the table of the English team, Blotto said, "Enrico me old shove-halfpenny board, I had a thought." This was a rare enough occurrence to command Twinks's full attention. "You're a bit of an empty revolver in the transport department, aren't you?"

"It is true that I no longer have a car, yes."

"So, you're in a bit of treacle tin with regard to getting to Rome, aren't you?"

The Italian shrugged. "I suppose I can rent a car here in Monte Carlo."

"But that'd put you in the position of a Backfoot Billie. You'll be way back in the wash of the two stenchers you're trying to get revenge on."

"That is undoubtedly true."

"So why don't you muck in with us in the Lag?"

"But surely the weight of an extra passenger will slow you down?"

Blotto chuckled at the suggestion. "You clearly don't know the Lag. Load her to the gunwales and she'll still spring ahead as hearty as the heartiest hartebeest."

Enrico Parmigiano-Reggiano shook his head. "No, I cannot let you do this. You are already at sufficient disadvantage. You are kind to make the offer, but I will not allow myself to handicap you so."

"But —"

Twinks intervened. "That's very honourable of you, Enrico, playing the Galahad, and we appreciate it. But you're right, the weight of an extra body would weigh us down." Blotto, about to argue the point, was stopped in his tracks by a steely beam from the azure eyes, as his sister went on, "At the moment, though, we don't know where our chauffeur is. Should he not appear before the bully-off, you would be most welcome to accompany us to Rome in the Lagonda."

"Well, if you're sure . . ."

"Sure as a schoolboy's sniggering," said Blotto. "We will be clubby with the company, won't we, Twinks?"

"Yes, we'll be lighting the fireworks of fun with you in the car, Enrico. And, of course, when we get to Rome, you can show us the sights."

"It would be my pleasure," he said, focusing those dark eyes on hers.

Twinks smiled winsomely, then quickly recovered herself. "But only, of course, if Corky doesn't reappear."

"Of course," said the Italian, somewhat cast down.

"If he doesn't, though," she purred, "you and I can sit together in the back, Enrico."

Had he not already been won over, that would have clinched it. "Should your chauffeur not reappear, I will accept your kind offer with pleasure," he said.

"Splendissimo!" murmured Twinks, reducing Enrico Parmigiano-Reggiano once again to a poleaxed puppy.

With eight o'clock approaching, noise from the front of the hotel grew, as the Monégasque press milled around and their photographers took shots of anything with the Les Automobiles Carré-Dagneau colours on it. Though a few engaged with Blotto and Count Daspoontz, the real focus of their attention was the race's favourite, Florian Carré-Dagneau. The lead of two hours, twelve minutes and forty-three seconds that he had built up seemed, with only one leg to go, unassailable.

There was still no sign of Corky Froggett. When Blotto expressed anxiety about this, Twinks said airily, "Oh, he's probably chummied up with one of the hotel maids, who reminds him of the plumpilicious Yvette. Corky'll pongle the way to Rome under his own steam." Blotto seemed happy to accept this explanation, though Twinks was not as relaxed about the situation as she pretended to be. Given the Great Road Race's history of sabotage and dirty doings, she was genuinely worried about the fate of their chauffeur. But with the final leg about to start, she recognised that they had other, more pressing priorities.

So she announced that Enrico Parmigiano-Reggiano would accompany them in the Lagonda. Although the

160

rules of the Great Road Race dictated that Blotto should be sole driver all the way to Rome, his sister thought that having the Italian with them, for security and mechanical backup if required, was a sensible idea. Also, Enrico had lived in Rome all his life, and, in the later stages of the race, they might be grateful for his local knowledge.

None of the newspapermen showed any interest in the English team's change of personnel. Nor did any of them ask a single question about what was probably the biggest Great Road Race-related story of the day: the blowing-up of Enrico Parmigiano-Reggiano's Fettuccine roadster. Once again, Twinks felt certain that a great deal of money had been placed in the right editorial hands to ensure this lack of journalistic curiosity.

The start of the final leg of the Great Road Race was interesting. The competing cars, now reduced to three, were lined up across the road directly outside the Hôtel Huge. The press grew more excited as the start time approached, and the photographers went into overdrive. Ever the showman, Jean-Marie Carré-Dagneau had set up a cannon on the seafront to fire at exactly eight o'clock.

The moment the gun sounded — or, in fact, to be accurate, a full two seconds before the gun sounded — Count Daspoontz's Krumpfenbach Big Eight leapt off the grid. Blotto, being British, of course did not contemplate doing the same. He waited till the last reverberation of the cannon-shot had died down before easing the Lagonda into pursuit. He'd intended to take

161

this approach even if the German hadn't cheated. Having witnessed what the Krumpfenbach had done to the Cadebaker, he didn't want to be in front too early. He would choose the moment when he overtook his rival.

The strange thing, though, was the behaviour of Florian in the Carré-Dagneau Florian. Rather than shooting off with the others, the Frenchman stayed unmoving on the grid. He did not appear to be in any trouble, and indeed encouraged members of the press to come and talk to him.

"Presumably," said a very contemptuous Twinks, "that French thimble-jigger reckons his time lead is so long, he doesn't need to make an effort? Just arrive in Rome at his own pace and he'll still win the spoffing sovs."

"If the pot-brained pineapple thinks that," said Blotto, "then he's very definitely shinnying up the wrong drainpipe."

"No, there is something more serious going on," said Enrico Parmigiano-Reggiano, "I think we should be on our guard."

Twinks caught on immediately to his thought process. "You mean there's no way he's not going to be first across the finish line in Rome? He knows that he'll be taking the chequered flag?"

"Exactly. Seeing how much press his father mobilised in Monte Carlo, you can guarantee he'll have even more gathered at the Colosseum. And the photograph he wants plastered across the front pages of all the newspapers in Europe is not of an English or German taking the chequered flag . . . with news in small print somewhere beneath it that his son in the Florian won on time countback."

"Sorry, not even in the same country as you . . .?" said a bewildered Blotto.

"What Enrico is saying," Twinks explained patiently, "is that the Carré-Dagneaux have something up their sleeves. Florian is dawdling at the start, not because he thinks he'll win on time, but because he knows that, when he gets to Rome, there'll be no opposition in the way."

"No opposition?" Blotto echoed. "But we'll be there!"

"Not if the plans of the Carré-Dagneaux or Count Daspoontz work out," said his sister. "As Enrico says, we must be on our guard. Those four-faced filchers will stop at nothing to get their pics of the Florian crossing the winning line first."

The night Corky Froggett spent in the boot of the French car had not been the most comfortable of his life. But a man who had survived as long as he had in the trenches wasn't about to make a fuss. Instead, he spent the time planning the level of violence with which he would greet the unfortunate Frenchman who was first to open the lid.

He must have slept for a while, because he woke with a pain in his hip, where he must have been lying on some piece of equipment in the car's boot. Shifting his position alleviated the discomfort.

During the hours of darkness, he reckoned the compartment in which he was locked was sealed all around, but he did not experience any breathlessness. There was air coming in from somewhere and, as the Monégasque sun rose in the morning, he became aware of small vents in the sides of his prison, which let in a minimal amount of light.

That at least gave him the opportunity to examine the lock which was holding him imprisoned. But hopes of being able to release himself from inside were quickly dashed. The locking mechanism was contained in a steel box. He felt around the space for some implement with which he could possibly smash it open but found nothing suitable.

The only objects inside the boot, apart from himself, were the electrical equipment, which he was certain could prove the Carré-Dagneaux's responsibility for the bomb which had destroyed the Fettuccine roadster. He was also aware again of the strange metal cylinder that he'd noticed the night before. He explored its outlines with his hands. It seemed to be about the shape of, and not far in size from, a human torso. Maybe it was some replacement component for the Florian's engine, though it felt like nothing that Corky had ever before discovered in his long experience of vehicular engineering. He reconciled himself, for the moment, to not being able to identify it.

As the sliver of light from the vents grew brighter — though still not bright enough for him to identify the function of the metal cylinder — the warmth inside his

164

metal enclosure started to increase. Corky also grew aware of a rising volume of sound from outside. He identified its source as the pressmen who had been so much in evidence the night before, returning to cover the start of the Great Road Race's last leg. And he was faced with a serious moral dilemma.

His instinct, engrained, as Blotto had observed, by generations of serfdom, was to be supporting the Young Master and the Young Mistress. He should be with them in the Lagonda, fulfilling his duty as chauffeur and mechanic. All he had to do was to shout out, and someone would quickly release him from his metal coffin.

But, against that, Corky had to set how his release from the Florian's boot would look to the other competitors and the assembled pressmen. The Young Master, he knew, was a man of unshakeable integrity. Blotto had commented adversely on all of the skulduggery they had already witnessed in the Great Road Race. For his chauffeur to be found in one of his competitor's cars would immediately raise the suspicion that he had been in there to effect the kind of sabotage of which the other, less honourable competitors had been guilty.

Corky couldn't take the risk of the Young Master appearing to be a cheat. So, the chauffeur stayed silent, praying to the Almighty Duck that he was making the right decision.

Blotto's strategy for driving the last leg from Monte Carlo to Rome was, like most of his strategies, dictated

165

by his sister. Twinks told him to curb his instinct to go into the lead by overtaking the Krumpfenbach Big Eight at the first opportunity. "Don't forget what the stenchers did to the Americans' Cadebaker, Blotters. You don't want to get into a position where they can push you off the road."

"The lumps of toadspawn would have to catch me to do that. And there's no way the Krumpfenbach could best the Lag in a straight race. Besides," he went on, pleased to have found a new counter-argument, "we're taking the coastal route to Rome. There won't be any mountains for them to push me off."

"They could always push you into the sea," Twinks pointed out.

"Again, as I said, the running sores would have to catch me first."

"You will overtake the Germans when I tell you to, and not before!"

The echoes of the Dowager Duchess's tones in her daughter's voice chilled Blotto and ensured his abject compliance. "Good ticket, Twinks," he mumbled. "Whatever cooks your cabbage."

"Just do exactly what I tell you, Blotto!"

Enrico Parmigiano-Reggiano smiled with pleasure. He had always liked masterful women. They reminded him of his mother, with whom, like many middle-aged Italian men, he still lived.

Twinks drew a map from her sequinned reticule. "Meanwhile," she said, "I will check if there are any shortcuts we can take."

166

"I wouldn't don your worry-boots about that," said Blotto. "On this occasion we don't need your navigational skills."

"Why not?"

"We can take any route we like." Blotto tapped his nose knowingly. "Something one of the classics beaks at Eton told us. All roads lead to Rome."

Corky Froggett couldn't understand what was happening. The noises from the pressmen around Florian Carré-Dagneau's car suggested that the final leg of the Great Road Race was about to be started. The sound of the cannon firing and the sounds of the Krumpfenbach and Lagonda powering away seemed to suggest that the start must have happened. And yet he felt no movement from the Florian. Surely the Carré-Dagneau family had not thrown in the towel so near to the realisation of their dreams?

The next thing Corky heard was the opening of the Florian's door and the shifting of the chassis as its driver got in. Only one door had opened, so presumably the team's mechanics were still outside. Then he heard the voice of Florian Carré-Dagneau. The bittersweet time he had spent with Yvette had provided the chauffeur with sufficient French to understand the young man saying, "I will see you there, Papa."

There was a self-congratulatory laugh from Jean-Marie Carré-Dagneau, "Very good, Florian. And prepare to end your day taking the chequered flag at the Colosseum as the undisputed winner of the Great Road Race!"

Corky wondered what devious plan the cheats had in store for the next stage of their skulduggery. He stayed silent in the boot, waiting for clues.

Soon after the conversation between father and son, he felt the juddering of the self-starter, as the Florian moved off at a sedate pace. The air-vents were not big enough for him to see anything of their route but sounds from outside suggested that they were driving through the heavy traffic of Monte Carlo. As the car climbed upwards, the noise receded and the smell of vehicle exhaust gave way to fresher, more rural air. At the same time, the road along which the Florian was travelling became bumpier. They were definitely leaving the city behind.

This progress continued for some half-hour before the Florian came to a halt. The engine was left running, so Corky couldn't hear the details of an exchange between Florian Carré-Dagneau and another French voice. The sounds of heavy gates opening were followed by forward momentum of the car, which stopped again after a few hundred yards. This time Florian switched the engine off but did not get out of the car.

A few minutes later, Corky heard the sound of another powerful car approaching from behind. It stopped and the engine was switched off. He reckoned it must have been the Adélaïde, when he once again heard the voice of Jean-Marie Carré-Dagneau speaking to his son. "Get her in as soon as possible, and then we'll be off."

168

"Yes, Papa," Florian agreed meekly, as he pressed the self-starter.

Corky felt the car move slowly forward. Then, accompanied by shouts in French from outside of the "left a bit", "right a bit" variety, it started to climb up an incline. With a clattering of metal, it came to rest on a horizontal level. The engine was switched off, the driver's side door opened and closed as Florian Carré-Dagneau got out. This was followed by considerable shaking of the car's chassis, accompanied by the clanking of chains and frustrated Gallic swearing. The strange cylinder in the boot shifted, clanging against its walls and against its unwilling occupant.

The imprisoned chauffeur interpreted the cause of these disruptions as the Florian being strapped down to a metal surface, just as it had been on the trip from Dover to Calais. He couldn't make sense of it. Surely they weren't on another ferry? He would have sworn their journey had taken them northwards out of the city rather than down towards the harbour. And, besides, there was no seaside smell. Just the aromas of cold metal and oil.

Then everything went quiet for some minutes.

The next sound, when it came, was overpoweringly loud. Engine noise.

As he felt the container in which the Florian was immobilised move ferociously forward, gather speed thundering over a level surface and then seem to leave the road behind, Corky Froggett finally realised what was happening.

The perfidious French were flying the Florian to Rome in their Carré-Dagneau Giselle cargo plane!

CHAPTER
EIGHTEEN

Roman Roads

"Oh, surely I can overtake the stenchers *now*?" Blotto pleaded. They had negotiated Genoa, they had rocketed through Florence without taking in any of its architectural splendours, and now the Lagonda was on a stretch of wide-open road. The last sign they had passed told them they were ninety-eight kilometres from Rome.

Though "Why kilometres?" Blotto had asked, having already on many occasions expressed his opinion on foreigners' wilful use of the metric system. "It's just another example of them making things spoffing well difficult for themselves. For some loony-logic reason, they don't teach their children English when they're in nursery-naps. Then they drive on the wrong side of the road. And then they use these kilometre flipmadoodles rather than that Grade A foundation stone, the English mile!"

"In fact," his sister had pointed out on more than one occasion during their journey, "the mile was invented by the Romans."

"Well, I'll be jugged like a hare!"

"The word comes from *mille passus*. 'A thousand paces' in Latin."

Blotto looked downcast. The mention of the word "Latin" always took him back to endless after-school detentions at Eton. He and Latin had never bonded. In fact, they'd had about as much in common as the Titanic and a tadpole.

"Well, if the Italians invented the fumacious thing, why don't they spoffing well use it?"

"Because it was a very inaccurate measurement. The distance covered by a thousand paces would vary considerably, according to the length of stride used by the individuals making those paces. Not everyone's legs are the same length."

It was usually around this stage in his sister's explanation that Blotto lost interest.

"Oh, come on, Twinks me old carburettor, can't I overtake the lumps of toadspawn *now*?" Blotto repeated as they drew a couple of kilometres nearer to Rome.

Once again, she refused permission.

"Don't be such a candle-snuffer, Twinks. We're on the open road. The Lag's got more than enough power to zap past that Krumpfenbach and leave the Huns as Backfoot Billies. Who knows when we'll get the next window-crack to overtake?"

"I know," said Twinks definitively, "exactly where we are going to overtake the Krumpfenbach. When we're actually in the eternal City. Between the Piazza Margherita and the Piazza Quattro Formaggi runs the Via Pepperoni. But, because of the curve of the Tiber in that part of the city, the Via Pepperoni is not straight. It follows a broad loop. There is, however, a very narrow road called the Via Puttanesca which cuts off the corner. If the Lag is within ten yards of the Krumpfenbach when it enters the Piazza Margherita, and goes down the Via Puttanesca, it cannot fail to reach the Piazza Quattro Formaggi in the lead. Then it's foot down for the Colosseum and — splendissimo — we're all rolling on camomile lawns!"

"*Mamma mia!*" said Enrico Parmigiano-Reggiano. "I have lived in Rome all my life, but you seem to know the city better than I do."

Twinks shrugged. "Just a matter of doing one's homework," she said airily.

The Italian had the look of a puppy that had been poleaxed once again. Twinks was so far from being just a pretty face. Was there anything this magnificent woman could not do? He almost, momentarily, began to wonder whether he'd met a woman more powerful than his mother.

He watched as Twinks drew a pair of mother-of-pearl binoculars from her sequinned reticule and raised them to her azure eyes. She focused on the car ahead. "And don't assume that we're safe from Count Daspoontz and his *banditos* just by staying behind them. I can see quite clearly — they're carrying guns!"

"The four-faced filchers!" said Blotto.

"Keep your peepers peeled," advised Twinks. "I think the German jigglers have more devilment up their murdy sleeves."

Corky Froggett had never flown in an aeroplane before, but he wasn't in the best position to appreciate the experience. Locked inside one metal box, the Florian's boot, inside another metal box, the Giselle's fuselage, was not the ideal way to enjoy one's first taste of aviation.

Nor was he very comfortable in his prison. Apart from the metal cylinder that kept rolling against him, the same sharp-edged object which had dug into his thigh during the night was again causing him pain. He felt along the floor of the boot with his hands but still could not find out what it was.

The Giselle did not seem to have been long in the air before the engine note changed, and Corky realised that they were beginning their descent. Needless to say, there was no comparison between the journey time by plane and by road. He was determined that, somehow, when he had made his escape, he would publicly denounce the Carré-Dagneau family for the cheating ways by which they had attempted to deprive the Young Master of his rightful prize.

But at that moment, he could do nothing. Just lie there in the Florian's boot, with a metal cylinder constantly banging against him and the uncomfortable hard corner of something digging into his thigh.

Once she had spotted the German's guns, Twinks ordered her brother to keep a greater distance between the Lagonda and the Krumpfenbach.

"I'm not afraid of their thimbly little bullets," Blotto complained.

"No, but it'd be pot-brained to get coffinated unnecessarily," his sister pointed out. "The aim of the exercise is for us to be first over the finishing line at the Colosseum. Then everything'll be creamy éclair."

"Yes, but pop your peepers ahead, Twinks! The stenchers are now out of sight!"

Sure enough, the German car had followed the road round an abrupt hairpin into a narrow ravine.

"Rein in the roans, Blotters!" said Twinks. "Slow down!"

"'Slow down'? And let the stenchers get even further ahead?"

"Blotto, do as I say!" The undertone of the Mater's voice made him lift his foot instinctively off the accelerator. "I happen to know that this is the only bit of road between here and Rome where Count Daspoontz could spring an ambush."

"Oh, don't talk such meringue!"

"It is true," Enrico Parmigiano-Reggiano confirmed. "This is the scene of many ambushes by the PR."

"Who're the 'PR'?" asked Blotto.

"They are one of the Roman branches of the Cosa Nostra," the Italian replied. "'PR' is short for 'Pecorino Romano'. They are a vicious, heartless organisation who have no more respect for the life of a human than they do for the life of a mosquito. Both can be slapped out of existence without a moment's thought — or a moment's remorse. Here, where the road narrows up ahead, the PR have hijacked many lorries carrying gold bullion to the banks of Rome. If Count Daspoontz has plans to eliminate you and the Florian out of the Great Road Race, there is nowhere better between here and Rome to do the deed."

"So, what's our creamiest plan? Drive round the corner slowly to catch them with their drawers down?"

"Blotters, you're hardly going to catch them with their drawers down when you round the corner in a car this size — particularly since they're just waiting for you to pongle along."

"Fair biddles, sis. So, what do you suggest we do?"

"Stop the Lag here for a momentette. I'll check them out." Twinks climbed up on to the bonnet, then drew out of her sequinned reticule the periscope she had used in the dungeon of the Château d'Igeaux. She raised it high, glued her eye to the bottom end and reacted to what she saw. "The filth-fingerers!" she cried.

The image in the small mirror revealed that the Krumpfenbach Big Eight had been stopped in the middle of the narrow road. In front of it had been built a barricade of wooden trestles. Though the obstruction could be relatively easily removed or even driven through by the weight of the Lagonda, Twinks saw that there were other dangers. Leaning over the back of the open car were Count Daspoontz's two uniformed mechanics. Each of them had a pistol in his hand. It was a very simple ambuscade, but one that could have proved fatally effective had they driven straight round the corner.

Twinks relayed to the others what she could see.

"The stenchers!" cried Blotto. "Do you think they'd be prepared to shoot us in cold blood?"

"I'd bet a guinea to a groat those buckets of bilge-water are capable of anything," his sister assured him.

Enrico Parmigiano-Reggiano agreed. "I'm certain their plan is to put us out of commission, wait for the Florian and eliminate the French team in the same way. Then drive on to glory in Rome."

"Glory won by cheating," announced Blotto, "has about as much value as a trouser-press in a convent."

"True, Blotters, but I don't think Count Daspoontz is worried about details like that."

"Being honourable is not a detail," said Blotto as he got out of the Lagonda. "It is the bedrock on which the British Empire was built!"

He went round to the back of the car to get something from the boot and emerged carrying his trusty cricket bat. "I'm going to confront these out-of-bounders," he declared.

"But they won't think twice about shooting you," said Enrico.

"Let them try. I will bat away their bullets."

Twinks also got out of the car. "I am going to come with you. Even wretches as lost to civilised behaviour as Count Daspoontz will not shoot a Venus de Milo."

"Why do you say 'Venus de Milo'?" asked a puzzled Enrico Parmigiano-Reggiano.

"Because I, like her, will be an unarmed woman."

"Ah," said the Italian. "Then I will come with you, to afford you some protection."

"You don't have to, Enrico me old marmalade-stirrer."

"But I do have to," he responded, yet again the poleaxed puppy. His tongue was literally hanging out.

Blotto led the way. As he rounded the corner of the road, he saw the scene, exactly as Twinks had described it. And he heard the voice of Count Daspoontz saying in heavily accented English, "Take one more step und ve vill shoot!"

Undeterred, Blotto continued his forward progress. He did not hold his cricket bat like a weapon, just casually against his shoulder. To emphasise his insouciance, he started to whistle "The British Grenadier".

Two shots rang out, kicking up dust on the sun-baked road in front of his feet. He felt encouraged. He could not believe that the Count's uniformed henchmen were such bad shots that they'd miss him from that range. In other words, they were deliberately shooting to miss.

Twinks had now come round the corner into the eyeline of Count Daspoontz. "*Fräulein*," he hissed, "you will be very foolish if you take another step. Ve vill not hesitate to shoot you!"

"Puddledash!" said Twinks. "I'm not afraid of you."

Two more bullets dug holes in the road just in front of her elegant silk satin shoes. She continued to walk forward, speeding up a little, so that she was alongside Blotto.

"Ve are not making ze joke!" screamed Count Daspoontz. "Ve vill shoot first you English — and zen ze French team! Ve vill be ze vinners of ze Great Road Race!"

"I wouldn't be so sure," said Blotto. "Anyway, us shooting each other would just be a waste of

178

gingerbread. What we should be doing is knitting our noddles together to work out how we're going to stop the Florian."

"I hay told you how ve vill do zis. Ve vill shoot ze Frenchies as soon as zey arrive. Just as ve vill shoot you."

"I think Blotto's idea is a good one," said a new voice. Enrico Parmigiano-Reggiano had just stepped round the corner into the Count's line of vision — and into the pistol range of his acolytes. "The Carré-Dagneaux have clearly got some devious plan to get both the Krumpfenbach and the Lagonda out of the running. We should be working together to frustrate their little schemes."

This suggestion seemed more appealing to the Count coming from the Italian than it had from the Englishman. "Perhaps you hav a point. Vorking together is not something that comes naturally to me, though."

"No, but have a little thoughtette about it," said Twinks winsomely. "When we left Monte Carlo this morning, the Florian and its nappy-happy driver had a lead of two hours, twelve minutes and forty-three seconds. So, he's just idling along the road behind us, keeping out of trouble, confident that we're never going to make up that kind of difference."

"But I thought you said . . ." Blotto was about to remind his sister that she'd said the Carré-Dagneaux would have some devious plan to ensure their man was actually first to take the chequered flag at the Colosseum. But a deterrent look from the azure eyes dried up the words in his mouth.

"The French," Twinks went on, "organised an illegal roadblock outside Valence to give Florian that illegal advantage. I don't think we'd be stepping too far over the barbed wire if we organised a roadblock here, to send him off on a long detour, and give the Carré-Dagneaux a taste of their own tincture."

"Vot? Und not shoot him?" asked Count Daspoontz, clearly disappointed by the suggestion.

"I think it'd be a better fit in the pigeon-hole," said Twinks. "After all, we don't want to go around coffinating people for no reason, do we?"

The expression on the Count's face suggested that this was not a view he shared, but he said nothing.

"What we need to do," Twinks continued at her most business-like, "is to get the Lagonda the other side of the barricade, and then build that defence up, so that the Florian won't be able to get past it without enlisting outside help. We're miles from any human habitation here, so it'll take him hours to drum up the drudges. And if he tries to get to Rome by another route, the detour'll take hours too. So, we can consign Florian to the fail-folder, and make it a straight level race between the Lag and the Krumpfenbach."

Count Daspoontz was ready to accept this suggestion. So ready that Twinks's suspicions were immediately aroused. She felt certain that the German team had up their sleeves another plan to eliminate the Lagonda from the race. But now was not the moment to worry about that.

Enough of the pallet barrier was quickly dismantled to allow the Lagonda through to the other side, and both teams, the German and the English, set about building a barricade strong enough to stop the Florian's progress. Some nearby telegraph poles were enlisted to strengthen the blockade, and Twinks used the soldering iron she kept in her sequinned reticule to join together metal fence-posts which would reinforce the structure.

The job of building the roadblock added another half-hour to their journey, but they still felt certain their overall time to Rome would beat that of Florian Carré-Dagneau.

Or they felt certain of that until Twinks once again took the mother-of-pearl binoculars out of her sequinned reticule. She focused on the road ahead, as it meandered through the rocky hills of Northern Italy.

And she saw, at least a mile away, speeding down a side road, about to join the main carriageway, a familiar violet-coloured vehicle. Its top was open and its only occupant was Florian Carré-Dagneau. He did not need the help of mechanics for what he was increasingly thinking of as his lap of honour. (Twinks was not to know at that time, of course, that the side road led up to a primitive airstrip, where the Carré-Dagneau Giselle cargo plane had just landed.)

All she did know, as she told the other barricade-builders with bemusement was that: "Somehow that filcher in the Florian has managed to get ahead of us!"

CHAPTER
NINETEEN

The Fate of the Favourite

"Oh, surely I can overtake the stenchers *now*?" Blotto pleaded again.

"No!" said Twinks, once more in full Dowager Duchess mode.

"Can't I at least get a spoffing bit closer?" her brother wheedled. It upset him to be so far behind the Krumpfenbach Big Eight. At some curves of the road the German vehicle was out of sight for minutes at a time.

"No!" replied Twinks even more forcibly. "We know they've got guns — and we have to keep the windy side of their range. We'll make up the ground on the Germans when we get to the Piazza Margherita."

"Maybe," Blotto objected. "But we still don't know how far ahead the Frenchies are. What chance have we got of turning the tricks on them if we don't get past the Krumpfenbach?"

This was actually one of those rare questions to which Twinks did not have an answer, but all she said was, "Rein in the roans and keep your distance, Blotters, until I tell you to do something different."

Blotto gritted his exquisite teeth but did as he was told. Enrico Parmigiano-Reggiano was once again deeply impressed by the power of Twinks's personality. Maybe he had finally encountered a woman more powerful than his mother. Here was someone who had the answer to everything.

Had Enrico been able to scrutinise the workings of Twinks's brain at that moment, he would have found her less confident of her powers than he was. Blotto's question had troubled her. Though she had by now worked out how the Carré-Dagneau Florian had managed to steal a march on the other competitors — using an aeroplane was the only logical possibility — she still couldn't see a way of reeling the cheat back in. It now seemed almost inevitable that the French car would be first across the line at the Colosseum.

Corky Froggett tried desperately to think of a way out of his current gluepot. He tried to think what the Young Mistress would do in his circumstances. (He found this was often more fruitful speculation than trying to think what the Young Master would do.)

And, as he thought of Lady Honoria, he became once more aware of the pain of something digging into his hip.

And he finally realised what it was.

He thought back to the dockside at Calais. And remembered what the Young Mistress had given to him and the Young Master there. He reached round and drew the wallet out of the back pocket of his uniform trousers.

The first object he took out of it was the electric torch. Switching that on made it easier for him to inspect the rest of the contents. As Twinks had promised, there were some French francs. And, infinitely more valuable, a set of spanners.

Corky used the torch to examine minutely the interior of the boot where he had already spent half a day. His inspection confirmed the conclusion that he had made by fumbling around with his hands in the darkness. There were no tools in the boot. Any that the French mechanics might need were stowed somewhere in the main body of the car.

But, along the centre of the boot's floor was a raised panel which, the chauffeur's engineering experience told him, covered the main driveshaft from the engine in the front to the car's back wheels.

For someone with Corky's mechanical skills and a set of spanners in his hands, what he had to do next was obvious and simple.

He loosened the nuts which fixed the driveshaft's cover in place, and in a few moments had lifted it off, revealing the tarmac of the road beneath flashing past.

He didn't rush but used the torch to make a careful examination of the driveshaft. Though it employed the latest technology, it worked on the same principle as every other driveshaft he'd seen. The juddering column of metal transmitted the power of the engine under the bonnet to the axle of the back wheels. The junction between shaft and axle was fixed in position with nuts and bolts, easy to see because the newness of the vehicle meant they had not had time to get discoloured by dirt or rust.

Corky Froggett knew the potential danger of the manoeuvre he was about to undertake. He couldn't see outside, he had no idea whereabouts on the road the Florian was. It was quite possible that uncoupling the driveshaft from the axle would cause a serious crash. A crash that could prove fatal to someone locked in the car's boot.

But Corky didn't mind. It had long been his ambition to give up his life in the cause of the Young Master, and he would rarely have a better opportunity to make the ultimate sacrifice.

With a prayer to the Almighty Duck, he found the right spanner and started to loosen the nuts.

It didn't take long. Suddenly, the Florian seemed to have been picked up by a giant hand and slammed down on to something made of solid stone.

One effect of the impact was to force open the car's boot.

Corky Froggett stepped out unscathed. He looked towards the front of the car. The driver's side door had been wrenched off by the impact. He saw Florian Carré-Dagneau stagger out in a state of high bewilderment. The young man sat down on a small rock, his back to Corky, of whose presence he was unaware. Florian was demonstrably alive and not in need of medical attention.

Finally, the chauffeur realised, he had the opportunity to identify the strange metal cylinder which had been his companion in the boot for so long. He instantly recognised it as a piece of body armour, hinged at one side and with a clasp on the other. The fact that it was

185

inside the Florian told him that the Carré-Dagneaux were anticipating violence involving firearms. And if they were planning to defend themselves against such an eventuality, then so could he. He decided to take the body armour with him. As he lifted it out of the boot, he found it surprisingly light, clearly made of some modern alloy.

Corky looked around at the place where destiny had landed him, the northern outskirts of Rome. All was dusty and dilapidated, but ahead he could see the densely packed buildings on the hills of the Eternal City's centre. That was the direction in which he set out to walk. He noticed that the dried grass and herbal aromas of the countryside had given way to the smell of sewers.

CHAPTER
TWENTY

And the Winner Is . . .

The sight of the disabled Florian by the side of the road produced a cheer from the occupants of the Lagonda — as no doubt it had, a few seconds earlier, from the occupants of the Krumpfenbach. "Splendissimo!" said Twinks.

"Tickey-Tockey," Blotto agreed, as he slowed the Lagonda down.

"Why are you stopping?" asked Enrico Parmigiano-Reggiano.

"Must check if the poor thimbles in the car are in zing-zing condition. Smash like that could put a boddo in the sick bay."

"But you are losing time in the Great Road Race," Enrico persisted.

"Look, this may be difficult for an Italian to understand, but —"

"It's all right," said Twinks. "Not a single paltry pineapple in the car. They've pongled off somewhere. So, they can't have been badly crocked."

"Good ticket," said Blotto, pressing the accelerator back down to the floor. "All creamy éclair now. With the Carré-Dagneaux having got their toodle-oo ticket,

187

it's just a straight gentlemen's race between the two of us."

"I wouldn't be so sure about the 'gentleman' bit," said Enrico Parmigiano-Reggiano. "I'm sure Count Daspoontz still has some dirty tricks up his sleeve."

"An Englishman's sense of 'doing the right thing' will always triumph over any dirty trick!" Blotto's assertion, though sounding magnificent, did not, Twinks realised, stand up to historical scrutiny. Particularly when he added, "You have only to look at the history of the British Empire to know that."

Still, it wasn't the moment to point out such details. Instead, she said, "We'll have our eyes out on stalks like snails to watch for any more diddle-handling."

They were only a few minutes nearer Rome when Blotto suddenly slowed the Lagonda down again and started reversing.

"What are you doing?" asked Enrico.

"Didn't you see that poor droplet there sitting on a milestone?" He pointed to a dust-covered figure in shredded garments. "It's Florian Carré-Dagneau."

"Why're you stopping for him? After all the trouble he's caused you?"

"Can't let him linger all bliss-bereft on the roadside, can we?"

The Italian was of the view that that was exactly what they could do.

"No, no. Be beyond the barbed wire not to give him a leg-up on the last leg."

"But think of the time! The Krumpfenbach will be —"

"Sorry, Enrico me old salami-slicer, but sometimes a boddo just has to do the decent thing."

Twinks went into the front passenger seat, and the new occupant was stowed in the back with Enrico, a companion substitution of which the Italian took a very dim view. The young Frenchman was very subdued. He admitted that he was walking towards the Colosseum but seemed disinclined to contribute anything else to the conversation.

Twinks wondered idly what might have caused the accident that had immobilised the Florian. Still, there'd be time enough to find out such details after the race had been won. She felt gloomy, though, about the likely identity of the winner. Though always respecting her brother's Galahad tendencies, she did think giving Florian Carré-Dagneau a lift was perhaps a noble gesture too far. The extra body's weight must be slowing the Lagonda down. And the time they were going to save by taking the shortcut between Piazza Margherita and the Piazza Quattro Formaggi was, minute by minute, becoming less likely to get them first over the line at the Colosseum.

Blotto, seeming to sense the urgency, drove the Lagonda faster than ever through the dusty streets. And he found that Roman pensioners, carters and shopkeepers scattered at his approach just as satisfyingly as had the denizens of France or his own beloved country.

It was striking, though not perhaps surprising that, as they drove through the northern suburbs of Rome, they saw lots of red and white Carré-Dagneau banners.

There were also photographers standing behind their huge machines on many of the street corners. The Great Road Race was certainly getting maximum publicity. Twinks expressed uncertainty as to whether Jean-Marie Carré-Dagneau yet knew that his own representative — and the favourite — was *hors de combat*. Idly, Blotto wondered what was the French for *hors de combat*.

The presence of the photographers cheered Twinks. Though the Krumpfenbach appeared to have a healthy lead, she was still suspicious that the Germans might have another trick up their sleeves to put the Lagonda permanently out of contention. But she didn't think they'd take the risk of being photographed using firearms.

Every other form of skulduggery, though, the English team had to be ready for.

"Right," Count Daspoontz shouted over his shoulder to his stormtrooper acolytes (in German) as the huge Krumpfenbach caused at least as much mayhem on the streets of Rome as the Lagonda, "we want to get these English pig-dogs in the Lagonda permanently out of contention. But, with all of these cameras around, we cannot risk using firearms." (How clever Twinks was — as usual — to know exactly how their minds worked.) "So, we will use the Thing."

The acolytes nodded. They knew about the Thing and had really just been waiting for the command to use it. They liked using the Thing.

190

"In order to use the Thing," Count Daspoontz went on, "we will pretend that the Krumpfenbach has broken down."

The acolytes laughed. The idea that the Krumpfenbach could break down was a funny one.

"We will draw to the side of the road, we will open the bonnet of the car and look inside it, as if searching for a mechanical fault."

That got another laugh. The idea that the Krumpfenbach could suffer from a mechanical fault was also funny.

"Then we will set the Thing across the other side of the road. The Lagonda will see that the road is clear and surge ahead. Then we will activate the Thing."

The acolytes laughed even louder. Once the Thing had been activated, the Lagonda would not be going anywhere. Nor would its occupants. Ever again.

Just as the Germans had planned, when the Lagonda came round the corner, the sight of the immobilised Krumpfenbach Big Eight brought enormous cheer to the English team.

"Larksissimo!" cried Twinks.

"Toad-in-the-hole!" cried Blotto, communicating pile-driver force to the accelerator.

It was Twinks who noticed and identified the alien strip across the road. She had encountered such deadly devices in her extensive reading. They were not always called "the Thing" — more frequently a *cheval-de-frise* — but she knew the destruction they could wreak.

"Rein in the roans, Blotters!" she shouted vainly, knowing the Lagonda had too much momentum to stop in time. Even as she spoke, she pressed the release on the underchassis compartment, also knowing that she was too late to set up any of the disaster-evading apparatus that she had stowed in there.

She saw the evil grin on Count Daspoontz's face as he pressed the button. And she saw, as she knew she would, the row of vicious spikes spring up from the strip on the road.

Twinks placed her hand on Blotto's, clenched against the steering wheel, and cried defiantly, "Well, we've had some larks, haven't we, Blotters me old sponge bag!"

Then she closed her azure eyes and waited for the inevitable.

But, instead of the sound of the spikes ripping through their precious vehicle's tyres and chassis, she heard a loud metallic clang. Just before the Lagonda launched itself into the air, she saw a metal cylinder that someone had thrown in front of the mechanical *cheval-de-frise*. It was this that had acted as a launch-pad and sent their car flying over the savage spikes.

The Lagonda landed with as much grace as two tons of metal can on a stony Roman road. With a cry of: "That'll teach the out-of-bounders — we're in the lead now!", Blotto urged their magnificent vehicle ahead.

Cheated of their prey, the Germans leapt back into the Krumpfenbach Big Eight, and roared off in frustrated pursuit.

Corky Froggett felt a little shaken, but, as he picked himself up off the road, he reckoned he didn't have any bones broken. He was slightly disappointed not to have worse injuries, disappointed in fact that he hadn't literally been able to lay his life on the line for the Young Master and the Young Mistress.

Still, he consoled himself with his faith. The Almighty Duck was clearly keeping the ultimate sacrifice of Corky Froggett for another, more important, occasion. He felt blessed and protected.

And if anyone ever wanted a testimonial to the efficacy of the body armour he'd found in the boot of the Florian, he would be more than ready to provide one. A metal suit that could take the weight of a Lagonda without crushing the person inside it was certainly a good purchase.

Corky decided to keep the body armour on, as he continued his walk to the centre of Rome.

The Lagonda was approaching the Piazza Margherita at enormous speed, when Enrico Parmigiano-Reggiano announced, "I think you should let me and Florian out at this point."

"Why?" asked Blotto breezily. "No icing off my birthday cake if I give you boddoes a lift all the way."

"I was thinking of the photographs," the Italian explained. "It will look strange in all the newspapers of the world, if the winning English car has a couple of non-Brits in it."

"Also," said Florian petulantly (in French, of course), "if I am not going to be seen crossing the finish line in my own car, I don't want to be seen crossing it in someone else's."

"Erm . . ." said Blotto, who didn't understand a word.

"Enrico's bong on the nose," said Twinks. "Give that pony a rosette! Drop them here, Blotters."

Obediently, her brother brought the Lagonda to a halt at the roadside. By the time their two foreign passengers had got out, the Krumpfenbach had swept past, Count Daspoontz and his acolytes jeering at them in German.

Blotto looked in frustration at his sister.

"Don't worry," said Twinks coolly. "The Via Puttanesca shortcut will still have us rolling on camomile lawns."

"Tickey-Tockey," said Blotto, and once again powered the Lagonda's mighty engine.

All went exactly as Twinks had predicted.

As they entered the Piazza Margherita, they just caught sight of the Krumpfenbach shooting off down the Via Pepperoni. Rather than following the same route, Twinks directed her brother into a space between two blocks of buildings that didn't look wide enough to accommodate even a bicycle. This was the Via Puttanesca. With considerable pulling down of washing lines and overturning of fruit stalls, the Lagonda made it through the narrow alley at high speed.

And they found themselves, exactly as Twinks had foretold, in the Piazza Quattro Formaggi, where a huge

194

crowd of press and public had foregathered to witness the final stages of the Great Road Race.

Just as the English duo exited, going down the Via Capricciosa towards the Colosseum, they saw the Krumpfenbach burst in from the Via Pepperoni, a full square's width behind them.

The streets of Rome have witnessed many triumphal processions in their history, but not even Pompey the Great's could match the manic enthusiasm which greeted Blotto and Twinks's Lagonda, as it purred its way towards the finishing line.

Count Daspoontz and his team did their best to make up ground but — even if they'd had the power to overtake the English car, which they didn't — there was no space for such a manoeuvre in the narrow streets. The level of fury inside the German driver turned his face puce and threatened to blow off the shaven top of his head.

It was matched by the level of dismay in the expression of Jean-Marie Carré-Dagneau, who had taken upon himself the task of waving the chequered flag when the winning vehicle crossed the fmishing line. He, of course, knew nothing of the accident that had befallen his precious Florian (in his precious Florian). His wife and daughter looked equally angry and disappointed. It was not the Carré-Dagneaux's finest hour.

But, with such a huge crowd present, and with so many photographers on the scene, Jean-Marie Carré-Dagneau had no alternative but to acknowledge the rightful triumph. And bring down the chequered flag.

195

Blotto and Twinks, the English team, in their English Lagonda, had undeniably won the Great Road Race!

CHAPTER
TWENTY-ONE

Roman Racketeers

The tightness of the smile on Jean-Marie Carré-Dagneau's face as he handed over the chest full of ten thousand pounds in gold sovereigns would have made rigor mortis look relaxed.

The smile on the face of Blotto as he accepted the prize could not have been more genuine. Never had he looked more handsome and heroic than when he waved to the adoring crowd, reassured that the Tawcester Towers plumbing could be fixed in perpetuity.

Enrico Parmigiano-Reggiano and Florian Carré-Dagneau had by now joined the welcoming party, though the expression on the face of the latter required another adjective than "welcoming". He quickly joined the rest of his family, all of whom muttered darkly in French about the crushing of their dreams.

Count Daspoontz and his stormtroopers did not look any happier. They too muttered, in their case dark Teutonic imprecations.

"We must keep the peepers peeled till we leave Rome," Twinks whispered to her brother. "The end of the race does not signal the end of the machinations of this shovelful of shibblers."

"Oh, but surely, Twinks me old pumice stone, they must recognise that the best boddo won? And it's only sport, after all."

His sister was sometimes touched by the dewy-eyed innocence Blotto brought to the world. But at times she did feel she had to disillusion him. "I don't think this ladleful of lugworms have the same definition of 'sport' as you do, Blotters. Remember all of the filth-fingering they did to us over the last few days."

"Yes, but now the race is over . . ."

"Don't drop your face-guard for a moment, Blotters."

"Tickey-Tockey," he said. But he did think she was being a bit paranoid. Even the worst kind of sponge-worm at Eton would accept when he was beaten fair and square. Only the worst sort of stencher would question an umpire's verdict after it had been given. Still, it never did to argue with Twinks.

"What I mean," she continued, "is that these sovs won't be safe till they're tucked up in the strongroom at Tawcester Towers. Until that happens, we need to keep this chest on hawkwatch."

"But once we've dibbled it away in the secret compartment of the Lag, no one'll ever find it."

"Suppose they steal the Lag . . .?"

"What kind of sponge-worm would do a thing like that?"

"The kind of sponge-worm we're dealing with, Blotters."

"But won't it be safe in the hotel garage? With Corky to guard it?"

"What you fail to remember, Blotters, is that we haven't seen Corky since yesterday evening in Monte Carlo."

"I thought you thought he was sharing an umbrella with some Monaco Moll."

"I only pretended to think that, so that you'd keep your concentration on the road ahead."

"So, you think Corky's been abducted by a bunch of French fugworms?"

"I don't know whether they were French, but I'm pretty sure he's in danger."

"Corky Froggett — in danger?" asked a very alarmed Blotto.

"Never!" said an approaching voice.

They both looked up to see what looked like a very dusty water tank waddling towards them.

"Great Wilberforce!" said Blotto. "It isn't . . . is it?"

"Yes, milord," said Corky. "It is."

"Well, I'll be snickered! What on earth's happened to you, you poor old thimble? You look as if you've been run over by a spoffing lorry!"

This was not, of course, a million miles from the truth, but Corky Froggett was not the kind of man to boast about simply doing his duty. The Young Master and the Young Mistress didn't need to know about their good fortune, the fact that he'd been walking along the road to the centre of Rome just at the moment Count Daspoontz had activated the Thing. Nor did they need to know that he had hurled his armoured body on to the spikes just in time to stop the Lagonda and its occupants from being shredded. Those were not the kind of actions for which men like Corky Froggett expected praise.

"Well, you've missed the main feature here," said Blotto. "Fortunately, the Florian had some kind of mechanical bishup, so it was the Lagonda that took the chequered."

Nor did Corky think it appropriate to mention his involvement in the French car's exit from the contest. The generations of serfdom experienced by his family meant that he knew his place.

At that moment the group was joined by Enrico Parmigiano-Reggiano. "I gather congratulations are in order," he said. "You did brilliantly!"

"Oh, don't talk such meringue," said Blotto instinctively. Compliments always brought him out in crimps.

"Anyway, it is now evening," the Italian went on. He was right. Blotto and Twinks had been too preoccupied to notice, but the shutter of the Mediterranean night had dropped suddenly during the closing stages of the race. "And I think I should take you out for dinner to celebrate your victory. I guarantee I know absolutely the best restaurant in Rome — it is owned by a cousin of mine called Luigi. There I will show you the most wonderful food and drink that the Eternal City can offer. Come, shall we go there straight away?"

"Tickey-Tockey!" said Blotto.

But his sister was more cautious. "I think we should get the Lag into a safe place first. One hears rumours of a lot of four-faced filching in Rome."

200

"You are wise to be wary," said Enrico. "Regrettably, there is much organised crime here."

"The Cosa Nostra?" asked Twinks.

"No, the Roman branch of the organisation," said Enrico, looking around surreptitiously before whispering, "the 'Pecorino Romano', of which I spoke to you before. They are evil. They will stop at nothing."

"Then maybe we should stay with the Lag until we leave Rome . . .?" Twinks suggested anxiously.

"No, your precious car will be safe in the garage of the hotel. Everyone involved in the Great Road Race is booked into the Hotel Palazzo Mozzarella di Bufala Campana. It is owned by a cousin of mine called Giuseppe. He has an arrangement with the Pecorino Romano. They will not touch anything on his premises."

"Well, that sounds *perfectino*," said Twinks.

"And I'll be in the Lagonda to guard it," asserted Corky. "In the hotel garage. Just in case."

"It will not be necessary," said Enrico. "Nothing criminal will happen on Giuseppe's patch."

"I'll still be there," Corky Froggett growled.

"As you wish." The Italian turned to Blotto and Twinks. "Right, shall we be on our way to Luigi's?"

"Just give us a momentette," said Twinks. "Let us go to the hotel, get the car stowed, check in and have a bit of a titivation. After a day on the road, I know I'm not looking my best."

"It is hard to imagine," said Enrico Parmigiano-Reggiano, "that someone who looks so stunning at this moment could ever look better."

Blotto sighed. He'd heard so many such compliments addressed to his sister. He had become used to men falling for her like guardsmen in a heatwave.

Once in the garage of the Hotel Palazzo Mozzarella di Bufala Campana, Twinks suggested that Corky Froggett might be happy to get out of his body armour. They could put it in the under-chassis compartment of the Lagonda. Alongside the prize chest. It would not, they remembered, be the first time that the space had been occupied by gold dedicated to the preservation of the Tawcester Towers plumbing.

But Corky resisted the idea of taking off his body armour. "Rome's a dangerous city, milady. I'll feel happier keeping it on."

Twinks didn't argue. With Enrico's assurances as to the security of his cousin's hotel, and Corky in place as extra protection, she felt that the Lagonda would be safe overnight. And overnight was all that mattered. Having done the business by winning the Great Road Race, both siblings were keen to return to the haven of Tawcester Towers as soon as possible.

In his suite in the hotel, Blotto bathed and changed into evening dress for the dinner ahead. Then he went down to the bar to wait for his sister. There he found a barman of pleasingly cosmopolitan experience, who actually knew how to make Blotto's favourite cocktail, a St Louis Steamhammer. A couple of those, making their customary detonations in his brain, took the edge off the familiar tedium of waiting for his sister to complete her evening transformation.

202

When she did finally emerge, there was not a man in the world who would not have been dazzled by her gorgeousness. Except for Blotto. But he was her brother, after all.

Luigi's was everything that Enrico had promised, and more. Blotto, always properly suspicious of foreign food, was very confused by the concept of pasta. Meat and fish, he had known from birth, should be served with potatoes, not stringy coils of dough. But, after a couple of glasses of an excellent Chianti Classico, he found himself downing platefuls of the stuff with enormous relish. But, even as he ate the pasta — and felt rather daring for doing so — he knew it would never catch on in England.

His sister, meanwhile, was enduring a full-on charm offensive from Enrico Parmigiano-Reggiano. Though he had made no secret of the attraction he felt towards her, sharing the back seat of the Lagonda had not been conducive to romance. But now, with the Great Road Race finished, he could focus the full beam of his Latinate charisma on her.

Twinks, used to the rampant affection of amorous swains everywhere she went, did not take his attentions too seriously (though she did find him increasingly attractive). Blotto, used to hearing men praising his sister in extravagant terms, went on filling his face with pasta. Enrico Parmigiano-Reggiano, ever the optimist, continued to speculate about whether he had finally found the woman for whom he would be prepared to move out of his mother's house.

One thing Blotto did notice, with some disquiet, was the amount of bodily contact used by Italian men. Every couple of minutes, when another swarthy individual came across to their table, Enrico would rise and enfold the newcomer in a hug. A man hugging another man! Well, that was way the wrong side of the running rail. As Blotto and all his other muffin-toasters from Eton knew, touching another man was all right during wrestling or boxing, when you were trying to hurt him, but not under any other circumstances.

After each hug, Enrico would introduce the newcomer to his guests as another cousin. There seemed to be hundreds of them. Blotto reckoned that anyone plotting the Parmigiano-Reggiano family tree would pretty soon have to send out for more paper.

Chiefly to get him off the subject of her eye colour, Twinks asked Enrico for more information about the "PR". Her extensive recent reading had not just concerned the latest developments in aviation. Knowing she was coming to Rome, she had done some in-depth research into organised crime in the city.

"The Pecorino Romano," Enrico told her, "is one of the most notorious divisions of the Cosa Nostra."

Blotto paid attention. He had encountered the words Cosa Nostra before. In America. He was a bit hazy about the details but seemed to remember they were some kind of charitable organisation. Something to do with helping out Italian immigrants to the United States.

"They have fingers in every pie," Enrico went on. "If you want to keep a business open in Rome, you had better make sure you have paid the appropriate protection money to the Pecorino Romano."

"And how do the slugbuckets behave if you don't pay? What do they do to you?"

"What don't they do to you? Torture, beatings, shootings, you name it. If the worst that happens is that you are thrown into the Tiber with a paving slab attached to your ankles — then you are one of the lucky ones."

"Oh, lawkins!" Twinks looked around the crowded restaurant. "So, has your cousin Luigi paid 'the appropriate protection money'?"

Enrico's face creased into a broad smile. "Ah, no. Of course not. The Pecorino Romano do not mess with the Parmigiano-Reggiano family."

"So, you have immunity?"

"In a way, yes."

"Why? Have you just paid more protection money than anyone else?"

"No, no, no. Like many things in Italy, it goes back a long way. To when my ancestors were simple farmers in Sicily. There was a dispute about the ownership of an olive tree, which had been going on for generations. Three families claimed that it was theirs. Then two families agreed to work together and share the olive tree and its produce. Those two families were the Parmigiano-Reggianos and the people who founded the Pecorino Romano. From that time, there is an agreement that neither family will ever do harm to the other. So Luigi's restaurant here has no trouble, pays no protection money. The same is true of Giuseppe's

Hotel Palazzo Mozzarella di Bufala Campana. You are completely safe from the Pecorino Romano in both places, and anywhere else that is owned by the Parmigiano-Reggianos."

"And what happened to the poor thimbles in the third family?" asked Twinks.

"I'm sorry?"

"The family that wasn't part of the deal to share the olive tree and its produce. What happened to the surviving members of that family? Where are they now?"

Enrico Parmigiano-Reggiano smiled. "There were no surviving members of that family."

Once they left the restaurant, Twinks had expected the Italian to suggest going somewhere else with her. Without Blotto. But for a man who lives with his mother, such possibilities do not arise. He had no alternative but to offer to walk her back to the Hotel Palazzo Mozzarella di Bufala Campana. With Blotto.

Enrico said he would call for her at ten in the morning "to show her the sights of Rome".

"Oh yes, I'd like to see those," said Blotto.

"You will not be coming," said the Italian firmly. "Just your sister and I."

"Oh, broken biscuits," said Blotto. But he wasn't that worried.

Nor was Twinks. Her plan was that, the following morning, she, Blotto and Corky would be on their way back to Tawcester Towers long before ten. She didn't feel bad about abandoning Enrico Parmigiano-Reggiano. Women who had had as much experience of amorous swains as Twinks tended to be a little cavalier about abandoning them.

At the hotel entrance, Enrico kissed her hand, in the manner of a man who'd much rather be kissing another part of her anatomy. And then he left them.

In the foyer, Blotto said, "Plumping pillow time."

But his sister had other ideas. "I don't think we should wheel out the jim-jams until we've checked on the Lagonda and Corky."

Sleepily, Blotto agreed.

It was as well that he did. When they got down to the hotel garage, there was no sign of the chauffeur. The Lagonda's driver's side door was open. The secret compartment had been unlocked. And there was no sign of the chest full of sovereigns!

CHAPTER
TWENTY-TWO

The Low-Down on the
Pecorino Romano

They inspected the secret compartment. Also missing
was the suit of body armour that Corky had worn the
day before. But none of the equipment loaded in by
Ronald the Second Mechanic in the Savoy garage had
been disturbed.

Blotto sniffed. "What's that noisome niff?" he asked.

"That's where it comes from." Twinks pointed down
to a cube of some crumbly yellow substance which had
been placed in the middle of the driver's seat.

"And what's that when it's got its spats on?" asked
Blotto.

"It's a calling card from the fumacious thieves."

"Sorry? Not on the same page?"

"That object on the seat tells us who's got the sovs,"
said Twinks. "It's *pecorino romano!*"

"Don't don your worry-boots, Blotters," she said, as
they climbed up the stairs from the garage to the foyer
of the Hotel Palazzo Mozzarella di Bufala Campana.
"Enrico Parmigiano-Reggiano can reset the clock on
this for us. Remember, he told us about his family

having a special relationship with the Pecorino Romano. He'll get the sovs back quick as a lizard's lick."

She moved confidently towards the reception desk, behind which stood a moustachioed gentleman who bore a strong likeness to their host of the evening. "Are you Giuseppe Parmigiano-Reggiano?" she asked.

He nodded his head in acknowledgement of his identity. *"Sì, signorina."*

"We are looking for your cousin Enrico."

He looked baffled. "I am sorry, *signorina*. I do not have a cousin called Enrico."

"Yes, you do, by Wilberforce!" Blotto expostulated. "He walked us back here from dinner not half an hour ago."

The man's face was blank. "I don't know who you're talking about."

"Enrico," Blotto continued, exasperated by the hotelier's slowness of comprehension, "told us all about how you've got immunity from the dastardly doings of that bunch of slugbuckets, the Pecorino Romano."

All colour left the man's face and his hands trembled as he responded. "Nobody in this city has immunity from the Pecorino Romano!"

They went back to the restaurant but got exactly the same reaction. Luigi Parmigiano-Reggiano also denied having a cousin called Enrico. He denied having seen a man by that name dining in his establishment earlier in the evening. And his hands too trembled when the words "Pecorino Romano" were spoken.

As they walked back to the Hotel Palazzo Mozzarella di Bufala Campana, Twinks said, "I should have known he was a filcher all along."

"Who?" asked Blotto, never the quickest to identify a change of conversational direction.

"Enrico Parmigiano-Reggiano."

"Oh. Tickey-Tockey."

"There were enough pointers."

"Oh?" A silence. "Like what?"

"When his Fettuccine roadster was blown up in Monte Carlo, his mood hardly registered a ripple. A genuine car-lover would have been in total crimps over something like that."

"You're on the right side of right there."

"Then again, remember when Count Daspoontz and his *banditos* were about to shoot us on that narrow bit of road. It was when Enrico appeared that they stopped firing."

"You mean the Germans have got into a sidecar with the stencher?"

"That's exactly what I mean." Another memory came back to Twinks. The azure eyes sparkled fiercely as she said, "Also, when we were trying to avoid the *cheval-de-frise*, Enrico saw me open the secret compartment. So, he knew how to get into it!"

"The lump of toadspawn!" said Blotto, deeply shocked. "Are you saying that Enrico Parmigiano-Reggiano is chummied up with the Pecorino Romano?"

"No, Blotters. I'm saying that Enrico Parmigiano-Reggiano *is* the Pecorino Romano."

210

"Broken biscuits!" said Blotto. Which was a measure of the depth of his emotion. "So, if the Pecorino Romano have got the sovs — and Corky — how're we going to get them both back?"

"I'll have to have a thoughtette about that," said Twinks.

The night porter at St Raphael's College Oxford was not overladen with onerous tasks, particularly at night-time. During the day, some of the resident academics might go in and out past his lodge, to deliver lectures or hold seminars. And there was a certain amount of traffic from younger aspirants coming to share tutorials with the great brains of the college Senior Common Room, but not a great deal.

The night porter at St Raphael's College Oxford was aware of his good fortune. Conversations with men who did the same job for other colleges told him that. Because the great advantage St Raphael's had over the rest was its complete lack of undergraduates. All of its residents already had degrees — and in most cases many doctorates and professorships to go with them. And the people who came into the building for tutorials were all graduate students.

So, all the problems encountered by his fellow porters did not impinge on the serenity of the night porter at St Raphael's College Oxford. His residents did not involve themselves in destructive pranks. They did not have to climb in over the walls after the college had closed at eleven o'clock. When they got drunk — which they did with considerable regularity — they got drunk in the setting of High Table dinners or the privacy of their own rooms, and raucous behaviour rarely ensued. St Raphael's was an aspirational template for other educational establishments. A college can be a very civilised place if you eliminate the disruption caused by having students in it.

The night porter at St Raphael's College Oxford did not waste the vast expanses of leisure which his job afforded him. He was a great reader — not of the kind of texts which preoccupied the college's fellows, but of romantic fiction. He had been introduced to a diet of stories, in which people who are right for each other encounter various vicissitudes until they are reunited in the last chapter, by a girlfriend. She didn't last long, but his appetite for fictional romance was an enduring one. And there was nothing the night porter liked better, at the end of a long and not very arduous day, than to snuggle up in bed with some heart-warming tale of loss and rediscovery.

Late one evening, he was deep into another such saga — just at the moment when the obviously right man was telling the obviously right woman that he was too old for her — when the telephone rang. For this to happen after midnight was a very rare occurrence. He answered it immediately, and heard the voice of a young woman, who sounded to be in her twenties, asking to be connected with Professor Erasmus Holofernes.

Influenced by his current reading and knowing the Professor to be his sixties, the night porter at St

Raphael's College Oxford instantly made the connection. It took a moment before a very bleary and irritated Holofernes came on the line. "Whatever is it at this time of night?" asked the voice of a man who'd just been woken from deep sleep and been dragged from bedroom to study by the telephone's summons.

"I'm sorry, Professor, but there's a young lady on the telephone for you."

"Young lady? But it's the middle of the night."

"It's me. Twinks."

"Twinks!" Never had disaffection turned more quickly to delight. "How wonderful to hear you!"

"Great to hear you too, Razzy!"

His heart warmed by having facilitated this romantic rendezvous, the night porter at St Raphael's College Oxford asked if it would be appropriate for him to get off the line now.

"Yes, get off straight away!"

The porter did not mind this abrupt dismissal. He knew, from his extensive reading, that people in love only have eyes — and time — for each other. Willingly, he put down the telephone in the lodge, and went back to bed to join his fictional lovers with an age difference. He did not know how they would resolve their problem but he had complete confidence that, before the end of the book, they would.

The night porter at St Raphael's College Oxford was not to know that the bond between Professor Erasmus Holofernes and Twinks far transcended mere romance. The empathy they shared was not physical or emotional, but intellectual. For, despite being surrounded at St Raphael's by the cream of British intelligentsia, the Professor very rarely encountered a mind to match his own. Twinks's was one of the few brains with whom his own could engage on an equal footing. So, he was always enchanted when she made contact, and it was a point of honour for him to solve her latest problem or answer her latest query as quickly as possible.

"My dear Twinks," he said, "the quality of the telephone line suggests to me that you are calling from foreign parts."

"You're bong on the nose there, Razzy! I'm in Rome."

"And what can I do to help you in Rome?"

"I want to know about the Pecorino Romano."

"Do you refer to the cheese or the . . . criminal organisation?"

"The criminal organisation."

A sharp intake of breath was heard from the Professor. "You are talking, Twinks, about one of the most vicious and callous crime syndicates in the world."

"Yes, I know. We've heard a bit about their blunder-thuggery."

"How have you managed to cross them? What have the villains done to you?"

"They've stolen a chest containing ten thousand pounds in golden sovs and they've shuffled away our chauffeur."

"Is he a chauffeur you care about?"

214

"Very much so, by Denzil!"

"I'm sorry to hear that."

"Oh?"

"The chances of your seeing again anyone who has been abducted by the Pecorino Romano are extremely slender."

"You mean they might coffinate Corky?"

"They would do it as soon as look at him. The only thing that might give them pause is deciding which form of cruel death they would make him undergo."

"The slugbuckets!"

"You are dealing with an organisation which does not deal in compassion or morality."

"Well, listen, Razzy, Blotto and I are determined to rescue Corky. And reclaim our sovs!"

"You would be very foolish to embark on such an undertaking. To challenge the Pecorino Romano is to ask for certain death. And a particularly unpleasant kind of death."

"Don't talk such toffee! Blotto'll protect us. He'll have his cricket bat with him."

"Just his cricket bat?"

"No, he'll also have the pure soul of an English gentleman."

"That may not prove to be sufficient protection against the might and viciousness of the Pecorino Romano."

"It will be. Don't you don your worry-boots about us, Razzy."

"Well —"

"Anyway, the reason I'm toodling you on the telephonico is that I want some information about the Pecorino Romano. I'm sure you have some."

"Of course I do!" He felt appropriately riled that she was casting an aspersion on the quality of his research. "I have it to hand right here!"

There was a sound of piles of papers being riffled through. Twinks had a vivid mental image of the chaos of the Professor's study, the teetering piles of documentation that covered every surface, the paper labyrinth through which only he could trace a path, and the extraordinary accuracy with which he could, within seconds, lay hands on any reference he needed. Her mind's eye also saw the Professor himself, tufts of wild hair sticking out from his balding head, dressed undoubtedly in shabby pyjamas and dressing gown.

There were more sounds of scuffling, and cities of paper towers falling, before Professor Erasmus Holofernes announced, "Right, I've found my notes on the Pecorino Romano. Updated only yesterday. What information on them do you require?"

"Well, first, who is the leader of the Pecorino Romano?"

"As you know, Twinks, most branches of the Cosa Nostra are family-based. The family who founded the Pecorino Romano is called the Parmigiano-Reggiano."

"Is it, by Denzil?" She couldn't honestly claim to be surprised. The whole scenario was unfolding all too predictably before her. She mentally kicked herself for her gullibility.

"And the leader, the *capo dei capi*, is a man called Enrico Parmigiano-Reggiano."

"The four-faced filcher!" said Twinks. She didn't voice the disappointment she felt, the self-reproach born of knowing how easily she had been persuaded by Enrico's Latin charms. And how close she'd been to getting closer to him.

"All right, Razzy," she went on, "what I want to know now is, having stolen our sovs and kidnapped our chauffeur, whereabouts in Rome are these ladlefuls of lugworms, the Pecorino Romano, likely to have taken them?"

"Well, Twinks my dear, where you are wrong is in imagining that the villains would have kept their loot — and your chauffeur — in Rome."

"Oh, lawkins!"

"The Parmigiano-Reggiano, like many Cosa Nostra families, originated in Sicily. But a branch split off and moved north to Abruzzo in central Italy. You know of Abruzzo?"

"Like a baby knows the nipple, Razzy."

He must have heard the note of surprise in her voice that the question should have been asked and apologised quickly. "Sorry, Twinks. Forgetting who I was talking to there for a moment. You must forgive me. It's so rarely these days that I have the privilege of talking to someone of your intellect. Of course, I should have remembered — you know everything."

"Give that pony a rosette! And join the club."

"Thank you. Anyway, to continue with the Parmigiano-Reggianos . . . From their base in Abruzzo,

217

many family members relocated to Rome, where, in a series of very brutal gangland battles, they quickly saw off their rivals and took over all the criminal activities of the Eternal City. There it was that they became known as the Pecorino Romano, and one of the most feared symbols in Rome became a cube of cheese left at the scene of a crime."

"Did the Roman police do anything to curb the stenchers' activities?"

"At first, they tried, but after a while — and a very high casualty rate among their ranks — the police agreed not to lift a finger. All bought off, all in the pocket of the Pecorino Romano. In fact, now the tables have been turned, and the police actually pay *them*."

"How, in the name of strawberries, does that happen?"

"The Roman cops have done a deal. In return for protection money, the Pecorino Romano have agreed not to blow up any more of their police stations."

"The lumps of toadspawn!"

"Yes, they're all-powerful. But, though most of the family's criminal activities are focused on Rome, their links with Abruzzo remain strong. Their headquarters are in the Central Apennines. They have an impregnable stronghold there."

"And that's where they will have taken the chest of sovs?"

"I'd put money on it."

"Not to mention Corky Froggett, our chauffeur?"

"Yes." There was a sombre note to Professor Erasmus Holofernes's voice as he repeated, "Yes."

218

"You mentioned," Twinks began tentatively, "the Pecorino Romano's cruel methods of coffinating people."

"I did."

The Professor seemed unwilling to go further, so she prompted him. "What kind of methods?"

"They're all pretty ghastly," he admitted. "But the worst of all is called . . . 'The Giant Mousetrap'!"

"And how does that work?"

"It is the product of devious and sick minds. And they have the nerve to find it a source of amusement. In a sense, the name describes it exactly. You know what a traditional mousetrap looks like?"

"Block of wood on which a powerful spring is pulled back and released when the mouse tries to remove a piece of cheese?"

"That's the one. Well, imagine that built on a human scale. Rather than a six-inch bit of wood, you have a six-foot one. And, rather than a tiny crumb of cheese, they have a three-inch cube of the cheese from which they take their name. The Pecorino Romano use this method on anyone they take prisoner. The deal on offer is this: If the prisoner succeeds in removing the cheese without activating the trap, he is free and will be released back to his family. If he does not succeed, the bar is released and he is crushed to death."

"Oh well . . . Jollissimo of them to give the prisoner a sporting chance."

"What do you mean, Twinks?"

"It's not certain death, is it? Must be a fifty-fifty chance of getting out with your trousers intact. I mean,

219

canny mice do sometimes get away with the cheese from mousetraps, don't they? I'm sure there must be prisoners of the Pecorino Romano who manage to bring home the bacon — or perhaps I should say 'the cheese'?"

"No," said Professor Erasmus Holofernes dolefully. "No one has ever survived The Giant Mousetrap!"

CHAPTER
TWENTY-THREE

The Impregnable Stronghold

There was no time to waste. Blotto drove the Lagonda east through the night towards the Central Apennines. Fortunately, the moonlight was strong, but he would have been lost — in every sense of the word — without his sister's navigational skills. Professor Erasmus Holofernes had given her the longitudinal and latitudinal co-ordinates of the Pecorino Romano's impregnable stronghold. A compass, a quick glance at a map of Italy and Twinks's phenomenal memory had done the rest.

The roads they travelled over were rough and ready, often little more than stony tracks, but they made good time. The Lagonda drove majestically through innumerable tiny villages, none of which had any streetlighting, and all of whose inhabitants were tucked up in their beds. Even the cats and the cat burglars stayed out of sight, though the noise of the mighty engine did set a few wakeful dogs barking.

The further they got away from Rome, the hillier the terrain became, and after about an hour of driving, it was positively mountainous. "We're getting close now," Twinks breathed excitedly to her brother. "Larksissimo!"

Bearing in mind Professor Erasmus Holofernes's description of the impregnable stronghold, Twinks told her brother exactly which rock to park behind. "We should get out and point the peepers at the entrance," she said.

"Aren't we just going to drive straight in?" asked Blotto eagerly.

"No, I think that might be rouletting the risk," Twinks advised. "Surprise is the ticket we're after."

"Tickey-Tockey," said Blotto, as ever respecting his sister's superior assessment of a situation.

He followed obediently as she led the way up the scrubby slope to the nearest rocky outcrop. Both innately fit, and neither carrying a milligram of excess weight, they made short work of the climb. And, once they'd topped the ridge, from behind a line of tenacious shrubs they could see into a natural crater, whose description exactly matched that given by Holofernes.

Twinks extracted the mother-of-pearl binoculars from her sequinned reticule and focused them on the scene below. What she saw was a complete village, with rows of little cottages, a couple of bigger houses, a duck pond and even a church. (In common with many branches of the Cosa Nostra, the Parmigiano-Reggiano family were devout Catholics. They did not embark on any of their activities until they had the blessing of the Church.)

Unlike the sleeping villages through which they had driven, in the impregnable stronghold everyone seemed to be awake. Light showed through the windows of the cottages and blazed outside from many flaming torches.

Electricity had not reached such a remote location, even for an organisation as powerful as the Pecorino Romano.

The dwellings were spread around a central open space, a kind of village green, which was full of armed men, some eating and drinking, some just smoking. But from all of them rose a buzz of excitement, as though they were about to witness some major event. Twinks felt a sudden spurt of resentment, as she recognised Enrico Parmigiano-Reggiano amongst the crowd. The way the other men reacted to him showed him to be their unrivalled leader.

She turned the binoculars towards the entrance to the crater, a gap which must have been chipped out of the living rock. Huge studded oak gates denied access to outsiders. As further protection inside the compound, two Maxim machine-guns were mounted to cover the gates and to provide a fatal welcome to any non-Parmigiano-Reggianos who might try to enter. Blotto's suggestion of simply driving up to the entrance was clearly a non-starter.

Focusing the binoculars back on the centre of the crater, Twinks saw, in pride of place, the chest of sovereigns, which she and Blotto had won fair and square in the Great Road Race. The chest of sovereigns which was rightly theirs and which, she was determined, would soon be back in their custody.

To the side of the chest, though, she saw something more disturbing. Surrounded by torches, which cast a flickering, other-worldly light over it, was The Giant Mousetrap!

223

"What in the name of snitchrags are you doing, Twinks?" asked Blotto plaintively.

"You'll see."

"But isn't there anything I can do to help?" asked her brother. "I've got my cricket bat here." This was his suggested solution to most sticky situations.

"I may need a bit of heavy lifting in a momentette," said Twinks. "But otherwise just sit and watch with a zip on your lip. I need to tune up the old brainbox on this."

Obedient to his sister as ever, Blotto held his peace.

Twinks did not hurry as she removed what she needed from the secret compartment beneath the Lagonda's chassis. But she could not suppress a feeling of excitement. Developed from her reading about the experiments by Jacques and Louis Bréguet, Paul Cornu and Jacob Ellehammer, her prototype had been constructed in great secrecy in a disused Tawcester Towers stable. She did not yet know whether it would work in practice. But she did not let her excitement affect her actions. She controlled her breathing carefully as she went through the process that had involved so many long hours of planning.

The first task involved releasing the leather straps which gave her access to the Lagonda's bonnet. Blotto watched, clearly having great difficulty in stopping himself from saying anything. Once she had access to the mighty engine, Twinks uncoupled the driveshaft and attached it to the purpose-built system of gears that she had taken out of the secret compartment. She was glad to find that the measurements she had taken had proved to be correct. The power-relaying gears ran smoothly from the engine across the middle of the Lagonda's windscreen and fitted into the custom-made brackets which she'd attached to the car's roof.

Twinks then enlisted Blotto's help to fit the steel cradle she had designed to wrap around the car's mid-section and screw its topmost part into place in the middle of the roof. The end of the gearing system rising from the engine slotted neatly into the correct aperture, and when she had fixed the upright shaft in place, she felt the reassuring clicks of the transverse cogs locking with the upright ones.

The physical effort of containing his curiosity had turned Blotto's face almost purple under its thatch of blond hair. But still he kept silent.

"Right, Blotto me old sock-suspender," said Twinks, "could you step into the Lag and give the old self-starter a ping?"

Bewildered, Blotto did as requested. The engine purred into life.

Outside the car, Twinks was rewarded by the sight of the top of the shaft turning fast in the moonlight.

All she had to do now was to attach the rotors.

With Blotto beside her, very cautiously Twinks tested out her invention. It took a while to get used to the improvised dashboard that she had designed for the controls, but very soon the Lagonda was lifting off from the stony mountain road. As the great car dipped and swerved through the air, Twinks made mental notes of some refinements she would need to introduce for the next prototype.

But basically, the conversion of the Lagonda into a helicopter had worked. "Splendissimo!" she shouted out loud, as the airborne car, growing more stable by the minute, rose towards the ridge from which they had looked down into the Pecorino Romano's impregnable stronghold.

Down in the crater, the reason for the gangsters' excitement had now become clear. Corky Froggett was led out of a small shed, flanked by two Parmigiano-Reggiano desperados, and taken towards The Giant Mousetrap. He didn't look in too bad a state. Although he had fought like a demon against the band of thugs who'd arrived in the garage of the Hotel Palazzo Mozzarella di Bufala Campana, the body armour he'd kept on had preserved him from too much injury.

But any hopes that they might let him continue to wear it in the impregnable stronghold were quickly dashed. The body armour might have withstood the weight of the Lagonda crossing the *cheval-de-frise*, but regrettably it wasn't going to be put to the test against The Giant Mousetrap. If the bar of that sprang back on to Corky, he would only have his uniform to protect him.

The chauffeur knew full well how The Giant Mousetrap worked. His captors had left him in no doubt about that. They had told him with great relish about the challenge offered to prisoners who confronted it. Pick off the cube of cheese without activating the mechanism and go free. Activate the mechanism and die. They did not tell him the statistics of survival amongst those who were forced to take on the challenge, but he intuited that they weren't very high. In fact, he doubted whether anyone had ever survived.

Corky was reconciled to his fate, even eager to embrace it. He had, after all, always wanted to lay down his life for the Young Master and the Young Mistress, and his dream was about to be fulfilled. Also, since his spiritual experience at the Château d'Igeaux, he had become more at ease with the prospect of eternity. Though he would have had difficulty in articulating the concept, he had begun to wonder about the possibility of a kind of transmigration of souls. Was it possible that, dying after a life of chauffeuring, he might be reincarnated as a mallard? It bore thinking about.

He did not respond to the taunts of the Parmigiano-Reggiano family members who encircled him and The Giant Mousetrap. He felt above such raillery and was not about to return insult for insult. If he had happened to have a Vickers machine-gun in his hands, the response would have been very different. But he didn't, so he reconciled himself to death amidst the ridicule of the ignorant.

Enrico Parmigiano-Reggiano was clearly the leader of the gang, and he it was who led Corky towards The Giant Mousetrap. The chauffeur had little interest in the crowd around the contraption. They were all swarthy men, interchangeable with the desperados who had acted as mechanics in the Fettuccine roadster.

But he was surprised to see, in the middle of them, four faces he recognised. Jean-Marie, Adélaïde, Florian and Giselle — the entire Carré-Dagneau family! Corky did not have time to consider the full ramifications of their presence, but he got the main thrust of it. The Frenchies had been in league with the Pecorino Romano from the start. There had never been any question of the Great Road Race prize (after the Italians had taken their cut) ending up anywhere but back in the coffers of Les Automobiles Carré-Dagneau.

Enrico Parmigiano-Reggiano also insisted on spelling out, in English, the nature of the challenge that the chauffeur was about to face. This was clearly part of the ritual, and Enrico threw in, every now and then, a few words of Italian, which prompted raucous laughter from his acolytes.

Corky was now near enough to give The Giant Mousetrap a close inspection. He noted the size of the coiled spring which would bring the bar crashing down. He saw the position of the cube of cheese on its spike, too far away to be reached from a standing position. He saw the low metal hoop through which the victim would have to crawl to reach it, thus ensuring he was prone at the moment of cheese-removal. He saw, in fact, an instrument of unavoidable death.

"From the moment I say 'start' . . ." was the point Enrico Parmigiano-Reggiano had reached in his ritual. "From the moment I say 'start', you have one minute to retrieve the piece of cheese. And, as I say, if you are successful in retrieving it, for the rest of your life you are a free man, absolutely safe from any attacks by the

Parmigiano-Reggiano family. But if you do not make a move within that minute, you will be pushed towards the *pecorino*. And people who are pushed, unhappy experience has taught us, are almost never able to get the cheese without activating the mechanism."

Corky didn't know why Enrico bothered to say this. He felt certain that, pushed or not, no one managed to retrieve the cheese without activating the mechanism.

"I will count up to three," said Enrico Parmigiano-Reggiano, "and then I will say 'start'."

The crowd, their blood-lust up, roared approbation. Corky Froggett, focusing his mind on ducklike thoughts, moved towards The Giant Mousetrap.

"One . . ." said Enrico Parmigiano-Reggiano. "Two . . ."

The sound of the Lagonda's engine was one which Corky Froggett would recognise as readily as a mother would her baby's cry. But he had never before heard it coming from above.

He and the baying crowd looked up in amazement to see the great car descending towards them. Their scattering had the effect of clearing the perfect landing pad. Twinks, now mistress of the controls, brought the Lagonda down to earth without the smallest jolt.

At that moment, two things happened.

Enrico Parmigiano-Reggiano, anticipating the ruin of his murderous ritual, gave Corky Froggett a fierce push towards the cheese on The Giant Mousetrap.

And Blotto leapt out of the passenger side of the Lagonda, brandishing something in his hand.

Of course, the propulsion of Corky towards the cheese triggered the sprung bar of The Giant

Mousetrap, and his death by crushing seemed inevitable.

But, just before the accelerating bar hit the unfortunate chauffeur, Blotto inserted his upright cricket bat between it and the Mousetrap's wooden floor. With an earth-shaking shudder, the bar stopped inches above Corky's abdomen.

In the confusion that reigned around them, it was a matter of moments for Blotto to grab Corky, and for the pair of them to grab the chest of sovereigns. Blotto bundled that and the chauffeur into the back of the Lagonda.

"Come on, Blotters," shouted Twinks. "We need to be as quick as two ferrets in a rabbit warren. Get in the car!"

"Not without my cricket bat!" her brother cried.

And, leaping back to The Giant Mousetrap, with superhuman strength he pulled the precious willow from its savage maw. There was an ominous splintering sound as the bat came free. And a thunderous crash as the bar completed its trajectory on to nothing but the wood of its base.

Blotto leapt into the passenger seat, just as Twinks, who had kept the engine running, started the Lagonda's ascent out of the Pecorino Romano's impregnable stronghold.

By the time the gangsters beneath them had regathered their wits sufficiently to start shooting, the English aviators were well out of range.

But the engine noise had disturbed the denizens of the duck pond, who rose in angry clamour. As Corky

Froggett, saved — almost literally — from the jaws of death, looked out of the window, he saw, flying around the Lagonda, a flock of ducks. Across his features spread a beatific look, most often witnessed on the faces of Old Testament saints. Had he been familiar with the word "epiphany", he would realise he had just had one.

CHAPTER
TWENTY-FOUR

Bringing Home the Bacon

They did not go back to Rome. They had no reason to. And certainly no reason to court unnecessary danger. The presence of the Carré-Dagneau family in the Pecorino Romano's impregnable stronghold had confirmed a suspicion which had already been forming in Twinks's mind. The French had been hand-in-glove with the Italians from the start. Regardless of the outcome of the Great Road Race, the chest of prize money had never been destined to become the property of anyone other than the Carré-Dagneaux. And the carbon copy of the letter she'd found in the study at Château d'Igeaux had obviously been addressed to Enrico Parmigiano-Reggiano.

They had flown some miles west of the Apennines before landing. They wanted to be well out of range of vengeful cars pursuing them from the impregnable stronghold. When they landed on flatter ground, the Lagonda had quickly been converted back from a helicopter to a road-going vehicle. And Twinks spent much of the journey back to England refining the adjustments she planned to make when she got back to her disused stable laboratory at Tawcester Towers.

Their return through France was notable only for one incident. Under no obligation to follow a route dictated by the Carré-Dagneau family, they ended up spending one night of their journey in Rheims. Blotto and Twinks were dining in an excellent restaurant there, when Blotto heard a familiar voice at an adjacent table.

"*Garçon!*" it shouted. Then in English, "Need another magnum of the bubbles over here!"

Blotto looked across to see the familiar orb of Trumbo McCorquodash, dining lavishly with his two young cousins. The Old Etonian muffin-toasters greeted each other in characteristic style. "How's the old wagon trundling, Blotto?"

"As right as a trivet's rivet, Trumbo. You know the sis, don't you?"

"Honoria, enchanted. And you know these two? Cousins. Never can remember their names."

"Yes, of course." The cousins had put on a bit of weight in the few days since the siblings had previously seen them. Following Trumbo's dining regime for any length of time would no doubt turn them globular too.

"But uncage the ferrets, Trumbo me old soda-splasher," said Blotto. "Are you pongling your way back?"

"Back from where, Blotto me old fly-whisk?"

"Well, Rome, obviously."

"Rome?"

"Yes." Twinks joined the conversation. "We thought you might have got delayed by the wines of the Côtes du Rhône."

"Côtes du Rhône?" The rotund one sounded very confused.

"Trumbo, I thought we started out together, only a few days ago, me in the Lag, you in the Ben, on the Great Road Race, due to end up at the Colosseum in Rome."

"Oh, lordy-lordy," said Trumbo McCorquodash, bringing both hands up to his plump face. "Do you know, we completely forgot about that."

"How could you?"

"Easy, Blotters. We are in the middle of the champagne district, after all."

Because of the time of the ferry, which brought them back to Dover late afternoon, they booked a night at the Savoy before their return to Tawcester Towers. As they were approaching the hotel, with Corky Froggett driving, Twinks suddenly said, "Oh, lawkins! Do you know what I've got to do tonight?"

"No, Twinks me old milk tooth. What?"

"I've just remembered where I'm meant to have been. Where the Mater thinks I've been for the last week."

"Remind me. With the various frolics of the last few days, that's completely drained out the brainbox."

"I'm meant to have been at Craigmullen."

"Craigmullen? Where's that when it's got its spats on?"

"Craigmullen is a castle in Scotland. I told the Mater I was on an educational course there. So, I must spend this evening producing works of art to show her."

234

"Still not on the same page?"

"I must produce some water colours!" said Twinks.

"But water doesn't have any colour," Corky grumbled. "That's the thing about water."

The morning after their return to Tawcester Towers, Blotto and Twinks were summoned to the Blue Morning Room by the Dowager Duchess.

"Where've you been?" she demanded. "Remind me." She had never shown much interest in the whereabouts of her children. From the nursery onwards, so long as they were out of her sight, she had required no further details.

"I," lied Twinks, "have just returned from Craigmullen, near Inverness." Though scrupulously honest in most of her dealings, she had special rules for engagements with her mother. The Dowager Duchess had lied to Twinks repeatedly throughout her childhood, so her daughter had early on determined to give as good as she got.

"Craigmullen?" The Dowager Duchess's echo seemed to emanate from some vast subterranean cave.

"The Scottish estate of the Duke of Glencoe."

"Ah." A familiar sneer cracked its way across the Dowager Duchess's rocky features. It was the one she reserved for minor — and particularly regional — aristocrats. "And what on earth were you doing in the frozen wastes of Scotland, Honoria?"

"I was learning to paint water colours, Mater." Twinks held out the sheaf of works she had so painstakingly created in the Savoy the evening before. "Would you like to see some of my landscapes?"

"Good heavens, no!" boomed her mother, scattering the proffered artwork on to the floor. (It may be a point of interest — though not in this story — that the water colours were subsequently tidied up by one of the Tawcester Towers housemaids, who gave one of them to a boyfriend. Its journey from there is unknown, but it did end up sixty years later in a fine art auction at Sotheby's, described in the catalogue as "attributed to J. M. W. Turner". Needless to say, Twinks was as skilled at the art of water colours as she was at everything else.)

"The only possible useful purpose of Art," the Dowager Duchess bellowed on, "is to preserve portraits of one's ancestors. What person of any sense or breeding wants to have a picture of countryside hanging on their wall? You can just look through the window to see that. Incidentally, Honoria, why did I give you permission to go wasting your time on water colours in Scotland?"

"There was some thought, Mater, that at Craigmullen I might encounter the unmarried son of the Duke of Glencoe who, as I'm sure you know, owns all the bits of Belgravia which don't belong to the Duke of Westminster."

"Ah, yes," said the Dowager Duchess, with renewed interest. "So, where's your engagement ring?"

"I regret, Mater," Twinks replied, "that the Duke's son demonstrated his unsuitability as a marriage component."

"Really? How?"

"I was informed by the maid who was assigned to me at Craigmullen that the young man, when breakfasting alone, did not use a butter knife."

"Ah." The Dowager Duchess nodded approval of the way she — or rather a sequence of nurses and governesses — had brought her daughter up.

Twinks's answer had let her off the hook in a way that reflected admirably on her ladylike sensibility. The Dowager Duchess now focused her basilisk stare on her younger son. "And what about you, Blotto?" she demanded, in a voice which had chilled him since he first met his mother at his christening when he was three months old.

"Ah, well, Mater, I've been driving in —"

"I know where you've been. My question is: Did you win the Great Road Race?"

It was one of those rare occasions (countable on the toes of a two-toed sloth) when Blotto knew he could supply the answer his mother wanted to hear. He moved across to the door of the Blue Morning Room and tapped on it. Responding to the pre-arranged signal, Corky Froggett appeared, and the two men carried the Carré-Dagneau chest across the room. Like transatlantic explorers bringing tribute to a European monarch, they opened the chest to reveal its store of sovereigns.

So rarely was it seen, that the great rift which appeared in the bedrock of the Dowager Duchess's face might not have been recognised. It was a smile.

"Well done, Blotto!" she barked. "You have done really well . . ."

237

So unfamiliar was a compliment from the mouth of his mother, that Blotto felt a little heady. He thought he might faint from the shock.

". . . whereas most of the time you are completely useless," concluded the Dowager Duchess, thus restoring normal service in her relationship with her son.

One of Blotto's regrets about participation in the Great Road Race was missing the start of the cricket season at the beginning of April. When he returned, though, it was in full swing, so that sorted out his activities for the rest of the summer.

Some players would have abandoned the bat splintered by The Giant Mousetrap, but Blotto was far too loyal to do that. The relationship he had with the bat was closer than that he had with any human being, even Twinks. He took the injured willow to the groundsman of the Tawcester Towers cricket pitch, who ran a kind of hospital service for distressed cricket bats. After applying copious amounts of linseed oil and strapping it with a special tape, he reckoned the reincarnated bat was "good for a few more centuries". Many of which Blotto made during that season.

The spiritual experiences he had undergone at the Château d'Igeaux and on the Apennines stayed in Corky Froggett's mind, and he was determined to find out more about the religious significance of ducks. He even requested the Young Master's permission to pay his first visit to the Tawcester Towers library.

There, he spent a whole day consulting many tomes in the Religion section. He found that jackals had been sacred to the Egyptian god Anubis, that bears were associated with the cult of the Greek goddess Artemis, that cows were venerated by Hindus and Zoroastrians, and that in Thailand a white elephant was believed to contain the soul of a Buddha.

But, though he discovered that the raven is a significant deity of the Tingit people of Alaska, nowhere could he find any reference to a religious system that venerated ducks.

This was not necessarily a reason for him to cease his personal quest. The chauffeur was not deterred by the prospect of belonging to a cult of one. He still felt in a state of spiritual confusion.

But when, that evening, he saw that the Tawcester Towers chef had put roasted mallard on the below-stairs menu, Corky Froggett swallowed his religious scruples, along with the duck.

However, there was one more consequence of the Great Road Race which caused the chauffeur considerable shock. Corky was an enthusiastic reader of *The Illustrated London News*, and it was with a copy of the latest edition in his hand that he sought out the Young Master. As expected, Blotto was found in the stables, communing with his beloved hunter, Mephistopheles.

"Milord," said a very agitated chauffeur, "look at this!"

The double-page spread opened out in front of Blotto showed the familiar outline of the Colosseum in

Rome. The cheering crowds, photographers and representatives of the world's press were all there. Emblazoned all over everything were Les Automobiles Carré-Dagneau banners, just as they had been when the Lagonda took the chequered flag in the Great Road Race.

In fact, the photograph depicted the finish of the Great Road Race. But one major detail was wrong. The car taking the chequered flag was not the Lagonda, driven by Blotto. It was the Carré-Dagneau Florian, driven by Florian Carré-Dagneau.

And the caption read: "CARRÉ-DAGNEAU TRIUMPHS IN GREAT ROAD RACE! FRENCH CAR SETS NEW STANDARD IN MOTOR-RACING!"

"The stenchers!" cried Blotto. "They must have restaged the finish! That is spoffing well not what happened!"

"It's what all the readers of The Illustrated London News now think happened," said Corky. "And, given how many reporters there were from foreign newspapers, it's probably what the whole world thinks, too."

Blotto seethed. "The four-faced filchers! This is cheating on a monumental scale! Typical of the French! They wouldn't behave like that if they played cricket!"

"Well, they seem to have got away with it," said Corky. "We know what really happened, but so far as the rest of the world is concerned . . ." he gestured to the photograph ". . . that's what happened."

"But it's not true!" wailed Blotto. "Newspapers are meant to report what's happened, not make stuff up."

"In this case, milord, that seems to be what they've done."

"Yes, in this one case the slugbuckets have got away with it. But it'll never happen again."

"Are you sure of that, milord?"

"Of course I'm sure. News is news, an accurate report of what actually happened. Whereas this is . . ."

"Fake news . . .?" Corky suggested.

"You're bong on the nose there," said Blotto. "'Fake news' — hah, what a fumacious notion! Anyway, don't let's don our worry-boots about that. So long as there are boddoes around in the world with some basic sense of honour, it'll never catch on."

BLOTTO, TWINKS AND THE INTIMATE REVUE

Simon Brett

It starts innocently enough at the intimate revue absolutely everyone is talking about, *Light and Frothy*, where its glamorous star Frou-Frou Gavotte has rather taken the fancy of Blotto's school friend Giles "Whiffler" Tortington. But while Blotto and Whiffler wait for the star outside the theatre to take her to dinner, Whiffler is seized and manhandled into the back of a cab which then drives off into the night . . . leaving Blotto with the problem of how to rescue his kidnapped school chum. Naturally, he enlists Twinks's help, and the two of them encounter actors, singers, impresarios, revue writers, cockney showgirls and Scotland Yard's finest — and white slave traders, who succeed in abducting Twinks — leaving it up to Blotto and his trusty chauffeur Corky Froggett to save her before she's shipped off to foreign parts forever . . .

BLOTTO, TWINKS AND THE STARS OF THE SILVER SCREEN

Simon Brett

The Dowager Duchess of Tawcester knows America is full of wealthy young men, all of whom will fall in love with her daughter, the supremely gifted Twinks — and marriage to a Texan millionaire would solve the Tawcester financial problems once and for all. So, along with trusty chauffeur Corky Froggett, the intrepid Twinks accompanies her brother Blotto on his Californian cricket tour. On arrival in Hollywood, they are invited to a glitzy party where they are introduced to a firmament of Hollywood stars, directors and gossip columnists; but the mood of the party suddenly curdles with the breaking news that beautiful starlet Mimsy La Pim — the (former) love of Blotto's life — has been kidnapped. And Blotto is determined to make it his personal mission to rescue her . . .

BLOTTO, TWINKS AND THE RIDDLE OF THE SPHINX

Simon Brett

Yet another financial crisis at Tawcester Towers! So this time the Dowager Duchess decides to sell off family possessions long consigned to the attic. Drawn to an Egyptian sarcophagus decorated with hieroglyphs, Twinks starts to translate: "Anyone who desecrates this shrine will be visited by the Pharaoh's curse . . . " just as the family chauffeur prises the lid off. The curse of the Pharaoh is now upon Corky, and it's up to Blotto and Twinks to travel to Egypt to banish it!

THE DETECTION COLLECTION

Simon Brett

A superb collection of new and previously unpublished crime stories to celebrate 75 years of The Detection Club, a society whose first president was G. K. Chesterton. The mantle of presidency has subsequently passed to some of the most significant names in crime fiction, including Agatha Christie and Dorothy L. Sayers. This collection of stories features eleven of the best British crime writers, including Robert Barnard, Colin Dexter, Reginald Hill and P.D. James.